PRAISE FOR

MONSTERS AND OTHER TALES OF HUMANITY

"Dash's fast and furious debut collection of weird fiction focuses on the ways alienation can make someone become truly alien. . . . It's a broad array of characters and setups, but at the center of each story is a person who has been pulled away from their own humanity and is struggling to find any way back. . . . Dash's thoughtful psychological exploration and evocative prose impress. There are no easy answers on offer here, but there is plenty of heart."

—Publishers Weekly

"From tender hauntings to monstrous children and strange video games, this collection of short stories pulls together some of my absolutely favorite things, and Carla E. Dash really knows how to nail an ending. At times brutal and at times soft and lyrical, *Monsters and Other Tales of Humanity* is weird fiction with a darkest, most intelligent heart."

—Natalia Theodoridou, World Fantasy Award-winning author of *Sour Cherry*

"Carla is a new to me author and I love her writing style—crisp but evocative prose with just the right amount of detail and a lot of emotion. I originally planned to read one story a day but it was very hard to put the book down. Most of the stories have a speculative element in them that gives the collection a unified feel, yet they're used in such a way that the stories don't feel too outrageous while still tackling relatable. real-world themes and iss~~~~

—Marie Sinadjan, author of *Ju*

monsters
AND
other tales
OF
humanity

CARLA E. DASH

Meerkat Press
Asheville

MONSTERS AND OTHER TALES OF HUMANITY, Copyright © 2025 by Carla E. Dash

All rights reserved. No part of this publication may be used, reproduced, distributed, or transmitted in any form or by any means without prior written permission from the publisher, except in the case of brief quotations embodied in critical reviews and certain other noncommercial uses permitted by copyright law. For information, contact Meerkat Press at *info@meerkatpress.com*.

"A Puzzle by the Name of L," originally published in *Love Hurts: A Speculative Fiction Anthology*, 2015
"Monsters," originally published in *Kenyon Review Online*, 2017
"Somewhere Far from Here," originally published in *Polychrome Ink*, Volume II, 2015
"What Was Meant to Be Buried," originally published in *Fantasy Scroll Magazine*, 2016
"The Thing in the Water," originally published in *Dies Infaustus*, 2018
"Hack n' Slash #999," originally published in *The Fantasist*, 2017

ISBN-13 978-1-946154-91-0 (Paperback)
ISBN-13 978-1-946154-92-7 (eBook)

This is a work of fiction. Names, characters, businesses, places, events and incidents are either the products of the author's imagination or used in a fictitious manner. Any resemblance to actual persons, living or dead, or actual events is purely coincidental.

Cover and book design by Tricia Reeks

Printed in the United States of America

Published in the United States of America by
Meerkat Press, LLC, Asheville, North Carolina
www.meerkatpress.com

for my mother and father

for the mother and father

CONTENTS

A Puzzle by the Name of L 1

Monsters 13

Somewhere Far from Here 16

What Was Meant to be Buried 28

The Thing with the Stars 32

The Child Breathes 47

Are You Even Alive in There? 51

The Thing in the Water 61

A Pretty Flower for a Pretty Lady 64

Hack n' Slash #999 69

About the Author 111

A Puzzle by the Name of L

When Death knocks on Stephanie's door, she is wallowing in the aftereffects of her fiancé's death, trekking aimlessly through the boggy muck that was once her heart, her life, and wondering if this year, finally, will be the one that drains away what's left of her will to live. Also, she is working on a jigsaw puzzle. The interruption annoys her because, even though most of the cardboard pieces are lying in dark, senseless piles, the blue-black of the river has just started to distinguish itself from the blue-gray mist hovering above it. This is important, she knows. The turning point of the whole activity. The first step towards completion. Stephanie is something of an authority on jigsaw puzzles. She has been doing a lot of them in the two years since Hayden died.

Looking through the peephole, she knows the guy standing on her threshold is Death because he's wearing a billowing black robe and swinging a scythe back and forth at his side in short, fluid pendulum arcs. Also, there is something about his looks. Something ashen, unfinished. Something not quite existent. She thinks, *I should be afraid*. She stands perfectly still, unbreathing, waiting for the emotion to flood through her veins, but she feels nothing, so she opens the door.

"Boo," says Death. His voice is grainy, a new or seldom-used thing, but with a deep, languorous current running beneath it. It is a voice with potential, Stephanie thinks. The kind of voice that could sing arias, seduce in seconds, if only he'd give a little cough or clear his throat.

"You aren't a ghost," she replies.

"I'm not?" he asks, all innocence.

Stephanie slides her eyes down the length of his body, once, slowly, just to be sure. Black robe. Still billowing. Scythe. Still swinging. She notices as well that his chest is quite broad, but that his fingers are long and thin.

"Obviously," she says.

"Hm. Good to know." Then he smiles, straight and bone white, but fetching, charming, like a guy who just a moment ago scored the winning touchdown and is now posing for a photograph, his dad's proud, vicarious arm slung across his shoulders. "Can I come in?"

"No."

As he sticks out his bottom lip and rounds his eyes into pathetic, puppy-dog orbs, Stephanie thinks there is something familiar about the arrangement of his features—the alignment of his pupils with the corners of his lips, the tilt of his nose, the curve of his eyes. A name flitters through the depths of her skull but won't float to the surface.

"I'm losing my mind," she decides, says, and shuts the door in his face.

But when she turns, he is sitting on her living room couch, ankles crossed, arms folded behind his head, smirking. Again, Stephanie feels she should be afraid. She should call the police. Try to throw him out. But she's never been one to fight the inevitable. If he got in once, she figures he can get in again.

So instead she flings out an arm and says, "Over there is the kitchen. Down the hallway on the left is the bathroom, at the end my bedroom, never go in there, on the right another room, definitely never go in there. This, obviously, is the living room. The couch you're sitting on is where you'll be sleeping. Do you even need to sleep?"

Death shrugs. "Sure. You done with the tour?"

"Yes," Stephanie says.

"Great, because this place is giving me ideas." Death springs up from the couch and bounces over to a wall. "You've got a loose socket cover here," he says, prodding the plastic and the wires beneath. "Maybe you can stick a finger in. I doubt it'd do the trick, though. Maybe if you stand in a bucket of water at the same time? Or," he says, dashing to a window, "maybe you can jump through this, while it's closed, of course, for maximum effect. Looks like a long fall. What is it? Eighteen floors? Nineteen? Wouldn't be very much left of you. Maybe you can stick your arm through the glass, then drag it back and forth across the shards. Or, if bloodiness appeals to you, maybe . . . do you have knives?" he asks, shooting off to the kitchen without waiting for an answer.

Stephanie hears drawers jiggling and the clang of silverware bouncing around. Death reappears, holding two of the largest knives she owns like nunchucks or sai, one in each hand. He slashes graceful semicircles through the air, then drops into a fighting stance. "Or," he says, popping back into verticality, letting the knives fall carelessly to the floor, "if you don't like the bloody approach, maybe you can go the drug route." And then he's darting down the hall, opening and closing cabinets, mumbling, "Jeez, these are a lot of pills, you've thought about this before, haven't you?" and stepping back into view, a bottle curled in the crook of each arm and one shaking in his left hand like a maraca.

Stephanie stalks up to him, snatches the bottles away, glares into his foggy eyes—amused, but impersonal, uncaring—and grits, "I'm not going to off myself, asshole."

"Are you sure?" he asks, voice bland. "Because my presence here begs to differ."

Stephanie takes a deep breath and holds the air tight in her lungs to keep from responding childishly, turns her back, and walks down the hallway, footsteps measured and light. "Don't follow me."

"Oh? And why should I listen to you?" Death asks, arms folded across his puffed-out chest.

"Please. Just don't," Stephanie murmurs as the door on the right side of the corridor clicks shut behind her.

Death plops onto the couch, fingering the faded, matted plush. "Fine, but you're no fun. If you take your time with this thing, I'm going to get bored."

In the room, surrounded by potted poisons—*Atropa belladonna, Digitalis purpurea, Datura stramonium, Conium maculatum* and the like—Stephanie kneels in front of the windowsill and tips a watering can, attempting to spout liquid out of the porcelain jug at the pressure and volume her mother would, wetting the soil so it's just barely damp to the touch.

~~~

The next morning, Stephanie wakes cold. During the night, her tossing and turning has bunched the blanket around her arms and hips and pulled it away from her feet, leaving them exposed and icy. Her nose feels frozen, numb. The arrival of consciousness is a slow, difficult ascent, like swimming upward through a deep, viscous bog. There are moments when she doesn't think she'll ever reach the surface. That's okay. She doesn't care. She stops wanting to. She embraces the sensation of complete immersion, of floating, of sinking, of burning, oxygen-deficient lungs. But eventually, she rises. The thoughts rushing through her head like a school of wild fish begin to slow into sense. She can catch and examine them. She can dissect their beauty until there is nothing left but corpses in her hands. She sniffs, disappointed, and swings her legs over the side of the bed, slipping her toes into the fuzzy, carnation-pink slippers her mother bought her when she was a girl. They are too small and worn; Stephanie's heels hang three inches off the backs, and she can feel the cheap, industrial carpet through their jagged-holed soles. Hayden used to say, *Momma's girl.* But Stephanie doesn't allow herself to think about that, doesn't permit Hayden to shake his head, bemused, or grin around teeth digging into his lower lip, attempting to hold back a smile, in her head. Instead she spots the image floating up through her memory from a distance, coalescing as it rises, and shoves it back under, dissolving it into harmless, sodden pieces.

Stephanie stretches and shuffles down the hallway, past the faded, flowery wallpaper she hates but doesn't have the motivation to change, because, one way or another, she'll be gone soon. The living room is drenched in a shade of cool white. Through the open curtains, she can see it is snowing. Heavy flakes cascade down in front of the glass. The ground is a river of white. The sky an ocean of silver. She frowns. *Another winter.*

Death has been snooping through her things. Books are askew on shelves, cabinets are open, picture frames full of sunshine and Stephanie's old life—she and Hayden on a beach in Hawaii, his head in her lap, her hands tangled in his dark, curly hair; she and Hayden, lounging under a white umbrella on a beach in Brazil; her mother, kneeling in her rose garden, light bouncing off her shears and seeping into her wavy tresses—sit erect on surfaces they usually lie flat upon. Stephanie itches to turn them down again, but refrains.

She can't see Death over the back of the couch, but his robe is draped over one of its arms, and his scythe, so dull and subtly curved Stephanie wonders if it would even cut her if she ran a finger across its edge, is propped against the side, so she figures he must be there. She wonders what he wears under the robe, if he's naked, what his body looks like. She peers over the top of the couch. He's wearing black cotton boxers and a white undershirt. His legs are hairy. His arms are thin, but defined. She thinks perhaps his complexion is a little more brown and a little less gray than it was yesterday. He looks ordinary, familiar.

"Throw yourself in front of a bus. Hang a noose from the ceiling fan in the kitchen," Death mumbles around the cushion his face is smooshed into. Stephanie sighs and he rolls over, rubbing his eyes.

"I'm telling you," he says, "I've thought about it. Broken bones jutting though your skin, blood pooling around your limbs, a snapped neck or a blue face, you could pull them off. They'd look good on you. You wouldn't be one of those hideous corpses. You'd be beautiful."

He yawns wide, stretches long and slow like a cat. Stephanie thinks, *how cute* quickly followed by *yep, I'm losing my mind* and pads into the kitchen to make tea. She pulls a China kettle down from a cabinet. It was a birthday gift one year from her mother to Hayden. Her mother never really liked him, always said she thought Stephanie spent too much time with him, neglecting her old friends and interests. But Stephanie knows the truth. Her dad was a deadbeat, uninterested and so long gone she doesn't have even a partial memory of his face, and there were no other children; she is all her mother has. When Stephanie told her she and Hayden were engaged, her mother relented, though. *Alright, alright,* she said. Stephanie was with her, walking through a flea market under a hot, blue July sky, when she bought the kettle, green and oblong, like a leaf, with embossed vines crawling along its surface. *Here,* she said, *Porcelain for the maker of dead things. Mom,* Stephanie said. Her mother sighed, *Alright, alright.* The memory of Hayden's dark fingers moving close to hers as they worked together to pull the floral wrapping paper away from the irregularly shaped pot bubbles up behind Stephanie's eyelids. But, as she runs water, watching the sink distort behind it, listening to it softly tap against the tarnished metal basin, sliding her fingers beneath the stream and feeling it slip silkily between them, the image sinks obediently beneath the surface of her thoughts once again.

When she returns to the living room, Death is sitting up, rubbing a hand over his face. Stephanie passes him a mug, decorated in concentric circles that lap like waves at the rim of the cup, and blows into her own matching one. Death perks up.

"Is it poisoned?"

"No!" Stephanie says, a little loudly, a little sharply.

"Aw," Death pouts. "So you're not going to kill yourself today either?"

"No."

"Oh, well. Hey! These are nice mugs. They look handmade. Did you make them?"

"No," Stephanie says. "My fiancé did."

"That him in all the photos?"

"Yes."

"What happened to him?"

"He's dead. Shouldn't you know that?"

"Lots of people die, you know. I can't be expected to remember them all. So? What happened?"

An image springs into Stephanie's mind before she can clamp down on it. The brown, flailing arms she sometimes imagines she saw sinking into the ocean in slow motion from the shore. The churning water. The swollen blueness of his skin when they finally pulled him out.

"He drowned," she says.

"And?" Death asks, eyes hungry, voice hushed and rapt. "What was it like?"

"I don't know," Stephanie says. "It happened fast. I don't remember."

~~~

Stephanie gets used to having Death around. He whirls through her apartment, causing chaos in every crevice, snooping, flipping through leather-bound photo albums and leaving them open on the carpet, running fingers over Hayden's bright ceramic cups, mugs, and baking dishes and discarding them on the Formica kitchen countertops, pulling her boxes and boxes of jigsaw puzzles off the rough, unfinished wood shelves that line the living room, turning them over, studying the pictures on the fronts, shaking them up, and replacing them in tall, precarious, asymmetrical piles. But Stephanie finds she doesn't mind. She has been alone for a long time and she is enjoying the little things about having a man around: the noise, the cooking for two, the picking up after someone else's messes.

One afternoon Stephanie is working on the jigsaw puzzle from the day Death showed up. She is agitated because as much as she wants to assemble it using deductive skills alone—as much as she longs to see only the size, shape, color, and pattern of individual pieces—she can't help but recall in perfect, vivid detail the scene on the front of the box. The dark water, the inky sky, the shadows of the trees on the distant shore, the motionless skiff and its obscure passenger all hover in her imagination with irritating clarity so that each jigsaw piece becomes a streak of water, a grain of wood, or a chunk of pine needles instead of a black, gray, or green sharp-edged, rounded, or protrusion-nubbed irregular polygon. Stephanie sulks, pushing the cardboard pieces around with the tips of her fingers, and tries to forget the whole to which they belong.

It is at this point that Death walks up to her, holding her cell phone delicately between the thumb and forefinger of one hand like he might a snake, by the head, cautiously, and afraid, as if he can't be sure he won't imminently suffer a life-threatening injury.

"What is it?" Stephanie snaps. "You want me to eat the phone? Beat myself over the head with it?"

"No," Death responds quietly. Stephanie squints at him.

"What then?"

"Did you know you have twenty-seven messages from your mother?"

"You've been listening to my messages?"

"Did. You. Know." Death snarls, slamming a palm against the flimsy, metal, foldout card table Stephanie uses for assembling puzzles. It squeaks and wobbles but doesn't buckle. Stephanie takes a breath, counts to thirty in her head, then pushes it back out.

"Yes, I know."

"Have you answered any of them?"

"No."

"Why not?"

"Obviously, I don't want to."

"But why not?"

"Why do you care?"

"I don't know. It's just . . . you used to be so close to her," Death says in a voice as smooth and deep as a bow sliding across the strings of a cello, a voice so familiar it hurts.

"What?" Stephanie asks, fear, shocking and novel, jolting through her diaphragm.

"Hm?" Death asks, eyes distant, distracted.

"How would you know that?"

"I don't know. It just feels true."

~~~

Incidents like this become the norm. Instead of greeting Stephanie in the mornings with gung-ho suicide suggestions like "a bullet between the eyes" and "roll around in a pile of glass shards," Death often begins the day with observations like "your hair is longer than it used to be" or "when did you stop running? You never used to be able to sit still." He wanders, glassy-eyed, through the apartment, dragging his feet and running palms across the ceramics in the kitchen, the fuzz of Stephanie's slippers, the gloss of photographs, and Stephanie knows he's recalling memories that aren't his. Sometimes he even reaches out and touches the top of her head, the side of her face, or the length of her sleeves, but Stephanie can't find it in herself to stop him or the wispy shivers that ripple through her limbs in the wake of his fingertips.

As for Stephanie, she spends increasingly more time in the room on the right side of the hallway and takes lots of baths, sometimes as many as three or four a day. Her bathtub isn't much, plastic and rectangular, no porcelain contours or lion's feet—an adjunct professor of horticulture, especially one who only works two out of three semesters a year like she does, can't afford to be picky about much when renting apartments—but she enjoys filling it to the brim, then tilting backwards beneath the surface and watching the world unglue. Vision blurs and sound distorts and she feels as though she's managed to remove herself from reality. She drifts away from it, unconnected, unaffected, but interested. A nonparticipating observer, an objective third party. She stays in until her body, pruned and waterlogged, becomes nearly too heavy to lift and her lungs burn from the effort of holding her breath.

~~~

Once, perhaps months after Death arrives—Stephanie can no longer be sure how long it's been; time flows past her, in front of her, and behind her, and she's not sure where exactly in it she is—Stephanie wakes abruptly and doesn't know why. She can't tell what time it is. The light filtering through the blinds is a hazy, gray-white, like cobwebs strung wall to wall, and could mean anything from early morning to evening or snowy midday.

Soon enough she hears rustling nearby, and when she turns her head, she discovers Death kneeling next to the bed, gazing at her. She considers becoming angry. She thinks perhaps she should remind Death of what she told him the first day they met—that he should never enter her bedroom—but she doesn't feel like fighting. She's sleepy and comfortable and Death's stare is a warm, gentle weight on her skin.

Time passes and Stephanie feels her body sink back into sleep. Her limbs become heavy, hard to command and hard to move. She dozes then dreams. The scene from her jigsaw puzzle appears. Stephanie is standing on the bank of the river in a cotton nightgown, mud squelching between her toes, fronds tickling her ankles, the skiff out in the distance. She has always been curious about that figure on the skiff. She watches and watches, peering through the fog, waiting for the silhouette to shift, for something to happen. No breeze blows through the trees. No mosquitoes buzz in the air. No waves beat the shore and the person on the boat sits as still as stone. Eventually, a hand reaches out. The fingers push together and bend, then dip silently into the water. When they emerge, cupping a handful of river water, they rise level with the figure's mouth, then tilt.

Stephanie wakes in a sweat. *Did the figure drink or not?* She doesn't know. Death's face hovers inches above hers, his hands trail across her forehead and down her cheeks.

"Are you alright?" he asks, breath ghosting across Stephanie's lips.

"Yes," she says, pushing his hands away, "I'm fine." He looks disbelieving but drops back onto the floor next to the bed. Stephanie focuses on the gentle burn his concerned gaze ignites in her abdomen and tries to slow the rise and fall of her chest.

"Do you remember," he says after a few minutes, "that time we visited the Pacific after we got engaged?"

"What?" Stephanie whispers, dread washing through her ribs.

"We went to California, to that beach. There were high, rocky cliffs. You were so happy. You kept smiling at me."

Stephanie curls her fingers into the cheap, stiff sheets pooling around her. "No, no. That wasn't you!" Death recoils, his eyes, a warm, light brown, Hayden's down to the most minute, golden flecks, going shuttered and unfocused. "That was my fiancé," Stephanie says more sedately. "You have to stop this. You aren't him."

"Yes. Of course. That's right," Death says, his voice rolling, wavering. "But do you remember anyway? When he took you there?"

Stephanie remembers. The water had been so blue, shot through with green and turquoise and bright, diffused sunlight. Hayden had been happy. Too happy. Too confident. He swam too far.

"No," she says. "I don't remember."

"Alright," Death says. "I made you breakfast. Have something." He lifts a tray from the floor beside him. On it are two pieces of toast covered in marmalade, eggs, a sausage patty, and a mug of tea. Suddenly Stephanie remembers the sorts of things Death used to say when he first appeared, things like "down a bottle of Oxycontin" or "chew up a death cap." There's no way she can force down any food he's made her.

"No thank you," she blurts.

"But—"

"Maybe later, okay? But can you leave me alone for a while right now? You're not supposed to be in here anyway. Please?" Death frowns, but turns Hayden's sad, soulful eyes away and acquiesces, drifting out of the room.

~~~

The next evening, Stephanie finishes the puzzle. Death is leaning against a wall, watching her as she locks in the last piece, a dark sliver of river. It looks exactly as she always knew it would. Starless sky. Unruffled trees. Water devoid of motion. The boatman in the center, dark and distant. Obscure, unknowable, impossible to capture. Stephanie takes a sip of tea from one of Hayden's mugs. She spent a long time preparing it, adding just the right amount of sugar (one and a half teaspoons), and heating it to the perfect temperature (140 degrees). She has let it sit too long, though. Now it's cold, gritty, and bitter. Of course it is. Stephanie sets the cup down gently, still conscious of the fact that it is something Hayden made, and begins disassembling the puzzle, unsnapping the cardboard pieces and throwing them in the puzzle box with quick, frantic flicks of her wrist and jabs of her fingers.

"Why would you do that?" Death asks. "Why did you spend so much time putting that thing together only to take it apart?"

Stephanie throws the box at his face. Puzzle pieces bounce off his shoulders and rain down onto the carpet. Before Death can respond, Stephanie pushes back her chair, runs down the hall, and locks herself in the room on the right side of the hallway. But this time, when she spirals away from the door, Death is standing behind her. Pale moonlight streams through the curtains as she watches him take in the contents of the room. The tall, twisting, deadly plants crawling up and around the walls. The delicate flowers blooming from their leaves. Purple bells of nightshade. Pink tubes of foxglove. Creamy trumpets of devil's snare. Fragile, white umbels of hemlock.

When Death faces Stephanie, his eyes blaze, with what—anger, desire, remorse, anguish—she can't tell. He slides forward, mouth, shoulders, and fingers tense, pressing their chests together. Stephanie's whole body pulses, with anger and something else she doesn't want to name.

"You aren't supposed to be in here," she says. "Go away."

"Shut up, you're so stupid, you don't understand, so just shut up," Death replies, then kisses her.

Stephanie is vaguely aware of clothes trickling away, of skin, of lips, of hands, of hips. But mostly, she floats, sinks, luxuriates in warmth. And it is good, great. The same pleasure as slipping beneath the surface of a hot bath except bigger, wider. A pool. A pond. A lake. A river. An ocean. A watery world. A viscous universe. She wants to drift down as far as she can. She wants to be consumed and come out on the other side. Or die.

Her senses stretch away from her. She doesn't feel the body above her, the carpet beneath her back, the sweat covering her body. Her limbs have become dead weight, heavy and immoveable. She doesn't see the walls of the room. She doesn't smell sex, or plants, or Death's breath breezing across her face. She can't hear a thing. There is no Stephanie. There is no Hayden. There is only darkness and stillness and silence.

~~~

When Stephanie wakes, the world is bright, sharp, and painful. The white sheets across her lap are so pristine they burn her eyes. The machines surrounding her whirr and screech. Jagged agony races through her abdomen.

A woman is hunched in a chair next to her bed. The woman's hair is limp, and her arms are thin. She looks worried, run-down, exhausted. The woman is Stephanie's mother. Stephanie is not surprised. Her mother always finds her eventually.

Through the hospital window, Stephanie can see blue sky and a portion of a thick Dogwood branch. It is covered in green leaves and small, pink flowers. She thinks, *another spring,* followed quickly by, *the time of year Hayden died.* When she cries, the heaves batter her ribs, the tears sting her eyes and scour salty tracks down her cheeks, and her throat and lungs feel rubbed raw, but still, she opens her mouth and breathes.

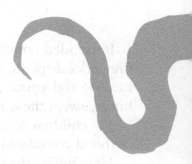

Monsters

Your children are monsters, the dying woman said. *How can you stand it?*

But what did she know? She didn't feel the fatherless progeny swirling in her belly, the last sparks of a husband who had been murdered in the street and left there, unfurled and oozing. She couldn't understand the way they churned and fizzed inside of me, promising that he would not be forgotten.

Or how they burst from me, ruining my womb for any children that might have come after. Or how they coiled tightly around my breasts like a cuirass, comforting and constricting. This she also didn't and couldn't know.

Mother, they whispered, sibilant and in unison, undulating against my ribcage, *whom should we kill?*

Those were their first words, these creatures so dark and iridescent. I had taken the last, beautiful starlight of my husband's life, nurtured it inside the caverns of my body, and these were the babes my prune-shrunk heart had birthed.

Now? I said. *No one.*

Why? they hissed.

Wait, I said.

And so they did. I sold my apples in the usual stall, on the street where my love had died. I stood shoulder to shoulder with neighbors on the train, letting their skin touch mine. I even smiled at their untroubled faces, though now I knew my body was nothing to them, just meat, unworthy of even a moment's passing empathy.

My children lashed their tails against my ribs.

When can we kill? they asked.

Later, I said.

I attended community picnics and town hall meetings and fireworks displays. My neighbors' children ran down the street, carefree and joyous. And when they fell, I brushed the dirt off their knees, swept the tears from their cheeks.

My children squeezed my sternum, but soon all in the neighborhood considered me a friend.

How unlike the rest of your kind you are, they said.

Meanwhile, others like my husband were killed by the tens, by the hundreds, by the thousands, in my neighborhood and out of it, while my neighbors carried on with their baseball games and their skiing and the mundanities of their undisturbed lives.

Now? pressed my children.

Wait.

It happened when I was walking home. A man knocked me into the street. I landed hard, scraping my palms red. I pressed them against the concrete, letting my blood dribble onto the ground where once my husband's had flowed.

The man told me to watch where I was going. The man called me a name that his people have flung at mine in hate for hundreds of years. The man laughed the superior, amused chuckle of someone who knew he was beyond the reach of my puny retribution.

You see? My children's forked tongues flicked against my skin. *He thinks you belong on your knees. This is what lurks in all their hearts.*

Yes. I took a deep, unfettered breath, relieved and bereft, as my children launched from my breast, howling.

They latched onto the man's eyeballs and twirled, burrowing straight through his head and out the other side. The man hit the ground, already dead.

My children corkscrewed on, toward the passersby who were just beginning to run.

No, I croaked. I reached for my children's tails, but they swung them viciously, whipping the air and my forearms. I pulled back, welted and stung.

They tumbled through the sky, roaring my name and my husband's, reaping their promised vengeance.

I stood. I walked away. Around me, my neighbors wailed. I

heard the most sickening sounds, but I did not look to the left or the right or down; I just stepped high when I needed to.

A woman grabbed my shoulders and shook me.

Your children are monsters, she said, breath rattling in her peek-a-boo chest. *How can you stand it?*

But she would never know for a great wind ripped her away before I could answer. A warm liquid misted my face. I kept walking.

My neighbors spared no thought for the seed of hate they planted in me as they let my love whither on the pavement, but I could imagine well the holes my children were ripping in families. I could feel, as if they were my own, the lives that would stop and not restart, the hearts that would never heal nor trust again, and the corrosive, self-consuming anger that would under no circumstances abate but just burn and burn under their breasts, poisoning every breath, corroding every interaction for the rest of their lives.

And so, at home, I prepared the things I needed—the chair, the rope—and stepped, just as they had stepped over the body of my beloved, just as I had stepped over them, for the last time.

Somewhere Far from Here

She'd rather go by the more beautiful Liza, or the stuffy Elizabeth, or the quirky Liz, or even the dull Beth, but the truth of the matter is this: the girl has never been called anything but Lizzie. She is new in town, and she rides the bus home from school. Today, like every day, it rattles over potholes, sending her flesh trembling on its bones. Still, Lizzie turns the pages of her weathered novel with care, touching only the tips of her fingers to the corners of the yellowed paper. The French words are jabberwocky to her, but she admires the book's looping calligraphy. From the etched pictures, she guesses she holds a copy of *Beauty and the Beast*. She discovered it on a shelf in the back of her last school's library, in the wrong place, wedged between two psychology textbooks. Lizzie is a good girl, usually, but she'd tucked the paperback beneath her shirt and left without a twitch. Lizzie likes to pretend the book is a treasure, an early or rare edition, perhaps the only of its kind, the sort of item that would cause a collector to sniff and caress, then close his eyes and whisper through reverent lips, *Exquisite*.

Lizzie turns the pages, stopping now and then to spread the book across her lap and peer out the nearest foggy window. The scenery is still only somewhat familiar; she has to watch carefully for her stop. The flurry of snowflakes whizzing past doesn't help. She is having trouble making out the few landmarks she knows: Dunkin' Donuts, the library, the violin store.

A half hour ago, as Lizzie listened to her history teacher drone, the sky was clear. But then she was in the city. Through her classroom's huge, industrial-grade windows, she watched municipal workers in tacky, plastic vests throw salt and sand on the sidewalks before the flakes began to fall. Bright yellow trucks stalked the streets ahead of time, like a pack of hungry wolves circling a sputtering fire, eyes aglow, jaws snapping, watering tongues lolling over the edges of their fangs. The blades of their empty plows dragged across the cement ground, grating, grating, grating so loud. Vile, Lizzie thought. Unpretty.

But here, on the outskirts of the city, until the bus muscles its way through, leaving bruised, crumbling mush in its wake, the snow lies where it lands. Lizzie likes that. It feels real, the way things would be if people weren't always pushing the world out of their way. It feels fake too, like something out of a fairy tale, but Lizzie likes that as well.

Around her, the bus is full of teenagers on their way home from school: couples covered in piercings, thrusting their tongues into each other's mouths; groups of girls screeching, laughing too loudly, and talking about shoes; guys with headphones draped around their necks, pumping bass through the bus; everyone saying the word fuck over and over. They are messy, inelegant. There are other people on the bus—men in suits, women with strollers, drunks—but they keep their heads down, or read books, or sleep. They hardly seem present.

Lizzie returns to her book. Usually, fairy tales soothe her with their magic, their steadfast sense of right and wrong, their flickering prettiness amid unceasing darkness. But today Lizzie is irritated. Her peers are scum. She is a nobody in a strange place, again. And how could Maurice let Belle take his place as the Beast's prisoner? How could anyone be such a coward? Lizzie's chest fills with disgust, an emotion that makes her want to slap herself.

Several miles from home, Lizzie pulls the yellow cord. The bus slides to a stop, and she disembarks. The driver yanks the doors closed. The wheels kick up piles of mauled snow, and then the bus is gone. Lizzie is alone, the smell of exhaust stings her nostrils, and she is cold. Goosebumps rise on her arms beneath her oversized sweater, but she doesn't mind because she can tell this neighborhood is a find. The snow falls soundlessly onto the old Capes and Colonials surrounding her, very different from the unceasing rows of ranch-style houses that populate the area her family currently calls home. She follows the tire tracks in the road, watching the wind animate the trees, every one older and taller than the houses in the yards they stand in.

For Lizzie, this neighborhood makes stepping into her most well-worn fantasy effortless. She pretends she's running, has run, away and that family, that monster with its talons sunk deep in her gut, can't hold her anymore. She opens her mouth and feels the cool flakes dissolve on her tongue. If there were more snow on the ground, she'd drop, roll, lie on her back, spread her arms and legs, and shape angels. She'd watch the flakes swirl in intricate patterns and cross her eyes as they landed, slushy, onto her cheeks.

And what would happen next? Would Lizzie be forced to spend the night on the streets, damp, splintery bench slats digging into her spine and cold seeping into her bones once night fell? Of course Lizzie doesn't think so. She imagines some kindly old lady would happen by, take one look at her, and say, *You, my dear, are coming home with me.* Lizzie imagines the heat of the fireplace the old woman would sit her down in front of, the salt-watery taste of the broth she'd feed her, the soft, fuzzy texture of the generations-old quilt she'd throw across her legs, the white of her hair, the flush of her cheeks, and the thick, sweet, molasses sound of her voice as she related the history of her family back and back and back.

When Lizzie comes upon the house, the fantasy dissolves. It is a solid, brick Victorian, ringed by a wrought iron fence whose spiked posts reach higher than Lizzie's head. It has square, asymmetrical towers, a steep mansard roof, gaping windows, and is large, imposing, and strange amongst the quaint homes surrounding it. Lizzie wonders why such dark, heavy curtains hang behind the windowpanes. She wonders why no lights glow behind the glass when the milky clouds have blotted the sun from the sky. A blacktop driveway hugs the house and slopes down and out of Lizzie's line of sight. She feels compelled to follow the driveway away from the street, so she does. She fancies there's something back there she needs to see. Lizzie cannot often indulge in impulse, but if she isn't home, if she is alone and no one is watching, she takes advantage. So when she comes to the dead end of a closed garage, she jumps the fence into the backyard.

A rusted shovel impales a patch of frozen dirt in one corner and a blue tarp covers something lumpy beneath a tree. In the center of the yard stands a treasure: a small, glass greenhouse, brimming with rose bushes covered in what Lizzie thinks are impossibly dark flowers. They are called Black Magic. Lizzie is captivated. The flowers are a dark, deep red, the color of coagulated blood. To Lizzie, they are beautiful, more red than black, like the last throes of sunset before darkness claims the sky.

Lizzie thinks the roses look like velvet. She wants to rub her fingers across their petals, hold the blooms under her nostrils, breathe in their perfume, and lie on the ground, surrounded by their branches. She wants to go inside the greenhouse. She tries the handle, jiggling a little harder and a little harder until she must admit it's locked. Then she kicks the glass and spins around, intending to search for a key or a sufficiently large rock. Instead she sees a curtain fluttering in a second story window.

Lizzie feels the blood pulsing in her throat. She wonders if someone is home after all, if he saw her, if he is a disfigured monster with a raging temper. She wonders if he will come outside to confront her. She wonders what she will do, how she will escape in time if he does. Lizzie holds very still and waits, but nothing happens.

~~~

Lizzie eases the door shut, places her backpack on the floor, then unlaces her boots and slips them off. On her way to the kitchen, she looks into the living room. It's not completely unpacked yet. Things are missing: family photographs, the embroidered pillows that are supposed to lie against the arms of the sofa, her mother's knickknacks. All her stepfather's model boats are out, though. Gray light glints against the glass jars that contain them. The room is immaculate. No half-full cardboard boxes litter the floor. There are no piles of objects yet to be placed. A visitor wouldn't know the room isn't as it should be. Her stepfather's work, no doubt. Lizzie glances back at the door to make sure her things are to the side, out of the way. They are.

Lizzie's parents are seated across from one another at the dining room table. Her mother sits rigid-backed, staring at the wall opposite her, hands folded neatly in her lap. Her fingers are shaking, a little bit. Lizzie can see the purple bruise on the inside of her left arm where the IV went in the last time she was in the hospital. Lizzie's stepfather is reading a naval history book, probably memorizing the names of the most masterful ships so he can order miniatures of them later.

"It's inconsiderate to make people wait like this, Lizzie," he says without looking up.

"I'm sorry," Lizzie says, demurely, ignoring the way the diminutive grates on her nerves, a physical sensation, like knees dragged through gravel. Her stepfather nods, satisfied. He's in a good mood.

"Well, what are you waiting for Claire? Go get the food," he says, flipping a page. And Lizzie's mother does.

During the meal, Lizzie watches them, her stepfather's tie twisted into an impeccable knot, her mother's lipstick unsmudged and bright against her pale skin, looking pristine, raising their wine glasses to their mouths just so and she, trying to remember which spoon to use when and on what, feels so far from lovely she doesn't know how she can stand it.

Lizzie is watching her stepfather cut a clean line down the center of his steak, listening to the way the metal of his knife slides against the porcelain plate beneath it, when her mother speaks. Unless her stepfather is the one talking, dinner is usually silent. "Avery, why don't we send Lizzie to stay with my sister for the holidays? Olivia hardly ever sees her. Plus, it'll give Lizzie some practice living without us for when she goes to college next year."

Lizzie isn't surprised. Her mother is always doing this sort of thing: suggesting sending her off to boarding schools, internships across the country, camps, relatives' homes: trying to get rid of her. It wasn't always this way. Lizzie remembers the times before her stepfather appeared when her mother would lie next to her in the dark, one hand gently twirling her curls, the other holding a *Little Golden Book* that she'd read under the glow of the plastic stars stuck to the ceiling. Lizzie remembers how, when the story was finished, her mother would kiss her forehead and say, *Goodnight, beautiful. Beautiful like Aurora?* Lizzie would ask. *More,* Claire would say. And little Lizzie would giggle, certain that as long as she was as pretty as a princess, everything would be okay in the end, just like in the books.

These days, Claire rarely looks at Lizzie. Now is no different. Lizzie's stepfather though, he drags slow, flinty eyes down her torso, appraisingly, like he's never properly considered her before, then glances at Claire's pinched face.

"Don't be silly," he says. "Lizzie's not going to college. She wouldn't leave us."

Claire's head springs up like a jack-in-the-box, eyes large and shocked. Lizzie tenses the muscles in her neck to keep her head from popping up the same way. In her peripheral vision she sees her mother's face, so pale, so white and pink, so different from her own, and recognizes her own emotions displayed there. She wishes her mother would shut her face.

~~~

Lizzie frequents the house with the roses. Sometimes she sits on the ground with her back to the greenhouse and her arms curled around her knees and stares at the curtain she saw move that first time. Sometimes she presses palms and nose against the glass of the windows at the back of the house, tilting her head and squinting, trying to see through the thin slice that separates the two halves of the drawn curtains, but it's no use. The interior of the house and its occupant remain a mystery to her. So she imagines. She thinks the house is probably a mess. Dusty cobwebs clog the corners. Soiled laundry clutters the floors. Sticky dishes pile up for weeks in the kitchen sink before the man who lives in the house manages to drag himself far enough out of his melancholy to wash them. And the man. She envisions him as young and handsome, but morose. He is an orphan. He has lost the love of his life. He is bipolar. Lizzie doesn't care what makes him hide away in the big, lonely house; she will make it better. Sometimes she imagines she will move in with him. The first thing she will do is open the curtains and let in the sunlight. The second thing she will do is make him smile.

But sometimes Lizzie hates the man who lives in the house. Surely, after the seventh or the twelfth or twenty-first time she jumped his fence, he must have noticed. And yet he never shows his face; he never steps outside to meet her; he never so much as leaves the greenhouse unlocked so that she can have a rose. And why not? Why shouldn't she get to own just one beautiful, improbable, winter rose when he hoards so many?

On a day when she is feeling this way, a day she has spent brooding over impending college application deadlines, Lizzie decides to break into the greenhouse. It isn't snowing, but the sky is that monochrome white of winter, like one enormous cloud without beginning or end. The house is still and silent, as always. The quartz Lizzie picked up from a ring of stones enclosing a stranger's yard weighs down her palm. Its rough edges scratch her skin and leave behind dry, ashy lines. As she cocks her arm and aims for a spot at the back of the greenhouse, a place she hopes the man who lives in the house won't notice right away, she thinks of her stepfather. She pictures the way he looked the night he announced she wouldn't be going to college—clean shaven, placid, imperious. Lizzie launches the rock. The glass shatters and shards hit the snow. The sound startles her even though she was expecting it. She examines the hole she has made. It is so small and jagged she isn't sure she'll be able to fit her hand through. A web of cracks branches out from its edges. Still, she slides her arm in. The glass presses against the soft flesh of her forearm, but doesn't break the skin as she stretches her fingers and closes them around the stem of one of the red, red roses.

Just as Lizzie manages to twist the stem forcefully enough between her thumb and index finger to tear it from the bush, she hears the metallic squeak of hinges and the thunk of wood hitting wood. She looks up. She can see a man's head, slightly distorted by the glass of the greenhouse, hanging out of a window on the second floor. Lizzie stares. His face is as pale as the snow on the ground. His hair, disheveled and as dark as the trim of the window framing him, falls across his cheeks and eyes.

"Hey! What the fuck?"

Lizzie's grip slips and thorns stab small, stinging gouges into her fingers, but she doesn't let go of the rose. The man ducks out of the window and Lizzie is sure he's coming to get her. She yanks her arm out of the hole, slicing a straight, shallow cut into her skin, from elbow to wrist. Blood drips onto the snow. She counts three drops before she sprints across the yard and hops the fence.

Blocks away, when her breathing has evened, Lizzie presses the flower against her face. She tickles her cheeks with its petals, sucks its dull, sweet fragrance into her lungs, and thinks about that beautiful, angry face in the window.

~~~

At home, Lizzie places the rose against her chest and zips her jacket closed around it before going inside. The thorns prickle her sternum. Her arm, concealed beneath her coat sleeve, has stopped bleeding. Her hand is bloody though, so she tucks it into a pocket. Her stepfather is waiting at the foot of the staircase, feet spread wide, and arms crossed against his broad chest. It is a testament to his anger that he does not think to reprimand Lizzie for failing to remove her coat and boots. Her mother stands beside him, squeezing her hands behind her back.

"Where have you been?" His voice is like the voice of a king. Lizzie doesn't dare lie. She doesn't dare tell the truth. It's the voice of someone so much more powerful than her, someone who holds her life between his thumb and forefinger and could snuff it out without so much as a passing thought of guilt. Keep pushing and I'll gobble you up, it says. Lizzie doesn't understand why he doesn't, why he hasn't yet. Lizzie's eyes dart to her mother's, rolling blue oceans of emotion she doesn't understand. When Claire bumps the accent table next to the staircase, it looks like an accident. It wobbles and so does the glass jug perched on top of it. Inside the jug is a delicate ship and glazed, blue clay meant to simulate waves. This is an expensive bottle ship, something Lizzie's stepfather bought on a business trip several years ago. Claire watches it fall, but doesn't move to stop it. She hisses as it bursts around her bare feet. Lizzie's stepfather turns on Claire.

"You. What did you do? What's wrong with you?" From past experience, Lizzie knows this is her cue to leave. She slinks to her room.

It's difficult for Lizzie to imagine at home; it's hard to take the shrill wails, rumbling commands, and occasionally meaty cracks for anything other than what they are. Still, in her room, she places the bloodstained rose on a windowsill and sits down at her desk to work on her personal essay. She's not worried. If there's one thing she can do, it's fabricate a story. She'll get out, escape to those tall, white towers covered in ivy, and never look back. There's nothing he can do about it.

~~~

When the rose withers, Lizzie returns to the house. Before she leaves, she stands in front of the full-length mirror in her room and does something she watched her mother do almost every Friday night before meeting her stepfather: spread color across her lips and above her eyes, run fingers down her hips, smoothing thin, shimmery material. The effect isn't the same, though. Not nearly for the first time, Lizzie scowls at her image. A brown tint runs beneath and bleeds through the surface of her skin, dramatic curves outline her body, and her tangled mess of frizzy curls more poof out than cascade down from her head. She isn't pale; she isn't thin; her hair doesn't fall straight and tame. He'll never go for her. He probably likes girls like Lizzie's classmates. The kind of girls that Lizzie sometimes watches in the locker room, tittering and pinching each other's thighs. They make her feel so foreign, so clueless, like she needs a guide to explain it all to her, these social habits of this other species. They also make her feel strange, exotic, but without the beauty, like something rare, but less than ordinary: a duck amongst a flock of swans.

Sometimes, Lizzie wonders if her life would be different, if she would feel some other way, if her father hadn't died when she was just an infant, if there were someone around who looked more like her. It's another of her well-exercised fantasies, trying to call into existence this alternate, shadow life. Claire used to keep a photo album filled with pictures of her first husband on a shelf in the living room, but it's gone now; purportedly misplaced by Lizzie's stepfather. So, no matter how hard she tries, Lizzie can never bring this life into focus. It grows wispier over time and eludes her grasp.

Lizzie tells herself the man who lives in the house is special and she won't feel like a duck with him. But here, even Lizzie runs up against the limits of her imagination and doesn't really believe it.

~~~

The man is walking out the front door when Lizzie arrives. She ducks behind an oak tree. It's damp to the touch and its roots are so deep and thick the sidewalk has cracked and bunched around them. The man pulls a pack of cigarettes from one pocket of his rumpled, designer jeans and a lighter from another. As he taps out a cigarette, Lizzie sees gooseflesh on the skin showing beneath the sleeves of his thin, gray T-shirt. He doesn't shiver, though. Lizzie is shivering. Her legs are bare and, underneath her coat, so are her arms and neck. But, staring at the man's thin fingers, his pink mouth, his dark eyes, she feels hot.

She doesn't notice the front door creak open at first. But when the man looks over his shoulder, so does she. In the doorway is a tousled, blond head. The head is connected to a naked torso, unmistakably male—Lizzie can see the definition of his abdominal muscles from where she stands—and flushed, with very pink nipples.

"You coming in soon?" The blond's voice is husky, raspy, like he's been screaming all morning. It sounds wicked to Lizzie's ears. The man with the dark hair hooks an arm around the blond's neck and moves in for a kiss. It is nothing. Just a brief, quiet slurp. Lizzie wants to throw herself across one of the house's spiked posts.

"In a minute," the brunet says. Now that he's not shouting at her, Lizzie loves his voice. It is not a cold, precise voice like her stepfather's, but a warm, nuanced one, like the surface of the ocean with the sun shining on it.

The blond disappears through the doorway. The brunet puffs a few clouds of smoke, then flicks away his cigarette and follows. Lizzie presses her face into the bark of the tree and cries, assaulted by the scent of mildew.

~~~

During lunch period the next day, Lizzie's cell phone rings. She is not in the cafeteria with everyone else; she's eating her soggy salad alone on the bleachers surrounding the football field. All those acne-ridden faces inhaling oily slices of pizza, their easy camaraderie, the brash, vulgar way they talk about sex—she couldn't stand it. A grape slides off the tines of Lizzie's fork, abandoned partway to her mouth. She watches a sparrow hop around the bruised, grounded fruit as the man on the phone explains about her mother's injuries.

Lizzie navigates the halls of the hospital with ease, though she has never visited this particular one; to her, hospitals are monolithic, each the same as or very similar to the one that preceded it. They've put her mother in a corner under a window. She is asleep, surrounded by humming, beeping, buzzing machines and what seems to Lizzie like miles of clear tubing. The wild vines of plastic plunge beneath the discolored flesh at her mother's wrist. Someone tucked a white sheet around her shoulders and Lizzie cannot tell the extent of the damage—whether she is merely bruised or if there are broken pieces this time—without lifting away the cloth. But she doesn't want to do that. The light beaming through the window creates tiny, firefly gleams on the tubing and her mother's cheeks. For a little while, it is beautiful.

Lizzie figures the police have already come and gone. They usually manage to show up when she isn't around. It's as if they know she wouldn't have the nerve to answer their questions, and they want to spare her the shame. By now, her mother has lied, and denied, and refused to press charges. From now on, it is inevitable that Lizzie's family will leave this place. Maybe next time it will be a different hospital and different police officers, but sooner or later people will notice. They will stare. Someone, eventually, will try to interfere. And then Lizzie's stepfather will pack his bottled boats, and they will move. Lizzie kisses her mother's pale, unblemished forehead, thinking of her most well-worn fantasy, slightly changed.

"I'll take you with me," she says. Claire doesn't stir. Lizzie isn't disappointed. She wasn't expecting anything else after all.

~~~

By the time Lizzie pushes her key into the front door, she's shaking. She can see the quiver in her fingertips, feel the tremors washing through her body in choppy waves. She clears her throat and hopes her voice will come out steady; she needs it to come out steady when she tells him.

On the trip home, Lizzie has imagined irrational scenarios. She expects to find her stepfather drunk and raging. She imagines that broken glass will pebble the floor, that he will have upended furniture and punched fist-sized holes in the walls. There's no reason for her to expect such chaos. Her stepfather is always cool, always in control, always methodical. Still, the sight of him seated at the dining room table, tweezing the ship Lizzie's mother damaged into a new bottle, is shocking. Lizzie expects the man who put her mother in the hospital to be more of a monster—wide-eyed, lank haired, pacing, pinwheeling his arms. But he is as normal as ever.

When he sees her, Lizzie's stepfather puts aside his project and folds his hands on the table. He asks Lizzie if she's okay. His voice is indulgent, like one adult comforting another over the death of a goldfish. When she doesn't answer, doesn't move, doesn't so much as breathe, he pushes back his chair and stands. He takes one easy, confident step toward her. Lizzie grinds her nails into her palms, willing herself not to retreat.

"I won't let you do this anymore," Lizzie says. "I'm going to go away. I'm going to go to college. Somewhere far from here. And I'm going to take my mother with me." Her voice holds firm. Amused, her stepfather shakes his head and advances.

~~~

Later Lizzie climbs the iron fence, slowly, painfully, because she's sore in the places she needs—arms, legs, thighs—and falls to her knees on the other side. A piece of cardboard has been taped over the hole in the greenhouse, but it's as effective as a Band-Aid on a gunshot wound. Cold air has oozed through, and the roses are dead. Some of the flowers droop from their bushes, dull, faded parabolas of red and green, but most are in pieces on the ground. Lizzie tries the handle. The door swings open, the roses apparently no longer worth protecting, and Lizzie lies down amongst the shrubs.

She knows what she should do. She should call the police and tell them what's happened. She even fishes out her cell phone to do it. But then she thinks about the things she'll have to relate, the words she'll have to say. They'll be like sludge on her tongue. Like sewage, like raw, rotting, dead things, like the gritty, slimy sweat she could smell pooling in the damp curves of her stepfather's body as he stood before her. Like the roses all around her, now more black than red. And they'll make her that way too.

She tries to dial the number. A number. Any number will probably do so long as she speaks. But Lizzie can't imagine the beauty in that so, sheltered by glass, dampness seeping into her clothes, thorns pressing into her sides, the thick, bittersweet smell of dying roses invading her nostrils, Lizzie closes her eyes and waits for someone to notice her.

What Was Meant to be Buried

I dreamed of dismantling him. He wasn't the first. I dreamed of dismantling others, too, before and after. But mostly him, for what he did to me when I was small, and we were meant to be gorging on chocolate milk and graham crackers while we waited the half hour for my mother to get home.

She never did believe it, my mother. But then, she never believed any badness about me. Not that I could suffer it. Not that I could perpetrate it. *She doesn't mean to,* my mother would say. *She can't help herself.* And always, always she was apologizing.

I didn't dismember him right away when I was big enough and strong enough and vindictive enough. For one thing, his relationship with mother had soured and we'd moved away. For another, I was still trying to please mother then. Everyone knows the worst thing in the world is abnormality, and I provided that in spades. She always thought it was her fault, something she'd done, a punishment. So I stopped lopping the heads off my dolls and bringing her delegged, desiccated insects. I took my meds.

And she rewarded me. With ice cream and coloring books. And later with lipstick and lacy, expensive bras. But also, with her regard. Her hugs, her smiles, her confidence and trust. We were best friends. She told me everything. Because if I was golden, so was she. Blameless, faultless, perfect. For a while, that was enough.

Sometimes I would slip. My mother would catch me dreaming of it, taking him apart the way I used to shred live moths and even once, covertly, a shivering, winter-doomed mouse.

What in the world can you be thinking of, wearing a face like that? She would ask, aghast, fist pressed to her jiggling, silicon bosom.

I would flatten my lips and narrow my eyes. Erase the smirk and the shiny, wide-eyed mirth. And then I would make something up. Something not gory. She knew. She must have known. But she accepted the lies, whatever they were. No matter how weak or unlikely.

But then my mother was dead, gone off to join my never-known and never-missed father. The police never could figure it out. The randomness of her death. The brutality. After, there was no one to stop me.

I buried what was left of him beneath the thorny vines behind his house. Later, I came back for the house. I liked the view. I didn't even need to dip into mother's bequeathal. Despite the convenient location and excellent shower pressure, the realtor was having trouble selling it. The locals were suspicious and superstitious. They jibber-jabbered, and I made out like a bandit.

In the spring, the vines blossomed. Heavy, star-shaped fruits bent the brambles near to the ground. I plucked one. The skin was golden like a Nilla wafer and lightly furred like a kiwi. In the kitchen, I sliced it into eights along the points of the star. The flesh inside was soft and pink and juicy. It was unlike anything I'd ever seen. Despite the unfamiliarity, I leaned against the counter and ate it. So smooth, so refreshing and sweet was the taste that I licked the juice off my fingertips like a cat.

I spent the night feverish and delusional, coiled around the low-flow toilet, vomiting. I imagined I saw my mother, rubbing her temples.

How many times must I tell you to mind what you stick in your mouth? she asked. And indeed, this was a childhood problem of mine, one I sacrificed to keep her happy.

"I'm sorry," I said.

She shook her head. *Why do you do this to me?* Or perhaps she said "did," for she rotted before my eyes, dropping into a pile of flesh and bones on the floor.

"I'm sorry. I'm sorry. Imsorryimsorryimsorry," I moaned into the porcelain.

I thought, too, that I saw him, the house's former owner, smirking in the corner, pleased with his revenge. Paltry revenge.

"You're dead!" I screamed, but he carried on chuckling and

pointing and leering, nudging the shoulder of another man I couldn't properly see. He was a shadow, more the shape of a man than a man truly. He radiated a feeling of sadness. My father perhaps?

It was this shadow man I most wanted to rend. For looking, for witnessing, for seeing what was meant to be buried.

In the morning, the fruit that had only yesterday been ripe and sweet lay rotting in the grass. I did not bother to throw it away for every day new fruit grew, ripened, and rotted.

Despite the night I'd suffered, despite the evidence lying in the grass, not eating the fruit was a trial. Still it hung, ripe and exotic on the vine. Still I remembered the juice running down my fingers as I bit into it.

I clipped a piece of the vine and tried to grow a second plant. If I could not eat it, I wanted at least to look on more of the beautiful fruit. The clipping took and the vine grew rapidly, but no fruit bloomed from its branches. The stars, it seemed, required particular sustenance.

The first vine continued its accelerated life cycle, and its decay drew animals. Scavengers scaled the fence and picked amongst the filth. Raccoons, crows, beetles. Their strong stomachs seemed to abide the fruit, though the corpses of other creatures, tricked by the ripe, still-on-the-vine stars, littered the lawn. Eventually, I ceded the territory. I gazed out the kitchen window, but stopped attempting to set foot in the yard.

Humans, too, were drawn to the sight. Neighbors stared, transfixed. They slowed as they passed, lowering their voices to whispers, gossiping as they held their noses. They had suspicions about the animal corpses, but none ever approached me nor I them. Until the stranger.

He had a lame leg, which he dragged as he walked. His flesh was covered in scarred-over burns, but also in bright, winding tattoos. It was hard to discern what was self-inflicted and what was not.

He followed his nose, limping around the perimeter of the house, and stood outside the fence, staring at my ripe and rotten fruit, my dead and living pets—for I had gotten careless about the back door and windows and now insects crawled in the sugar bowl and rodents curled on my rugs—not with revulsion, but with interest, as if he could look right through the blooms, inside the leaves, under the ground, and into the roots. He looked as though he could see, and was interested in knowing more. But no one was supposed to see.

He plucked a fruit and left. He did the same the next day and the next. He only ever took one fruit. He only ever took the tricksy, luscious-looking fruit. I grew curious.

One day I stood by the vine and waited for him, at his usual time, around noon. He thumped and thumped until he was standing just across the fence from me. He really was quite disfigured. But inside the ruin of his face, his eyes were human as were the tongue and teeth inside his mouth.

"Nice to see you up close and without a glass pane between us," he said. A hardhat was hooked to his belt. A house and a fire and a family twisted around his bicep. Everything about him was so on the surface. What kind of monster, I wondered, lay beneath?

One of the crows, the one I called Rook, landed on my shoulder and I drew my fingers down his spine. *Caw, caw,* he said.

"What," I asked, "do you do with the fruit?"

He picked a fruit off the vine and spun it by its stem. I noticed that there were many faces inked onto his skin. Names and dates hid amongst the elaborate designs that flanked the faces. Sandra 4/18. Janae 9/29. Mostly women, it seemed.

"Perhaps I like to eat them."

Rook picked through my hair, looking for grubs. I pushed his beak away from my scalp. *Caw,* he said.

"You must have a strong stomach. This fruit is poisonous."

"Worth it."

I thought of it, ripping him into little, inky, burned pieces. No better candidate. Mother would be so disappointed.

The man saw my lunatic expression, my sharp teeth and my big eyes, and he smiled with his twisted mouth. I noticed there was an empty, inkless space peeking out from the neckline of his T-shirt, above his heart.

"What is your name?" he asked.

And I told him, for I believe in fair play.

The Thing with the Stars

I don't think I noticed it right away, the thing with the stars, but I noticed it first. It was past two a.m. I know because when I crawled out the window onto the roof, I hadn't closed it behind me, which was stupid. Serena snatched the alarm clock off the nightstand and pitched it at my head. A little whirlwind spun past my ear and pinprick shrapnel exploded from the place where the clock collided with the window jam. Momentum kept it tumbling down the roof. I saw bright red numbers, and then the hatch popped open, and the batteries were flung, like ejected pilots, over the edge of the roof into the darkness, where gravity sucked them down to a splatty, alkaline-soaked death.

It was also the ass end of December. I remember because my father's birthday had been a week or two before, on the solstice, and when I was a kid, he liked to talk about it, how after midwinter, the days grow and the nights shrink. He thought it was something special, something that suited him. I think the solstice is night's last soothing dream before the sun, that star, that burning orb of some monster's eye, opens its reeking maw and starts tumbling hours and the people suffering through them around its playful palate, nipping with giant, blunt teeth as they pass—dizzy and blinded by the light flashing irregularly through their gaping, flesh-and-bone prison—and not spitting them back out properly until March. Nothing to be proud of there, Pop.

I'd celebrated the way I usually do: with beer and mail stealing and a foul mood. Serena had circled me on light, careful feet, but spun faster and closer every day until we ended up here, two bodies colliding. *Smack.*

I was annoyed about the clock. It was mine. My clock. My

batteries. My roof. What right did she have to get so close she could touch them? Exert her force on them?

In the bedroom, Serena was all wrath. Her hair was a bloom of corkscrews around her head. Her eyes were narrow and lined with kohl. The kohl was not running because Serena was not crying. Serena never cries. It's one of the things about her that I . . . appreciate. She threw up her hands.

"Oh, sure," she shouted. "Run away. Just like your—"

I shut the window. Her words cut off as neatly as if I'd pushed her through an airlock. It didn't matter. I knew what she was going to say. *Just like your dad.* I should have known. You tell someone something in confidence because they read in a magazine that "communication is the key to a successful relationship" and then they throw it in your face the first time they get angry. I turned my back and hoped the closed window would keep us both safe.

The air felt as cold as a vacuum, but I was warm. Jets of heat gushed through my belly and chest; blood flowed through my veins like magma.

I was having what you might call a bad day. At work, my stupid boss, that twerp with the moon-round glasses and skinny limbs, had been riding me again about my sloppiness and inefficiency, like anybody gives a shit what a mailman looks like or how he gets his job done.

After work, at the bar, I'd started a fight. No big deal. No cuts, no bleeding; I probably wouldn't even have any bruises. I'd just felt like a fight, so I'd pushed a guy, and kept pushing until he'd pushed back. I'd won. I win all my fights. And then, Serena, my girlfriend or not girlfriend or whatever Serena thinks she is to me, had been waiting here for me when I got home. She'd wanted to talk, again, like the idiot she is, about getting married.

I looked for Orion and hoped Serena would leave. I wanted to see those three crooked stars across his belt and remember that, despite what I said to Serena about how one day she'd leave, or I'd leave, people can't just disappear, not really, not completely, not as long as you still remember them.

It was Pop who taught me about the stars. Whenever my parents fought, which was pretty much every time Pop came around, sneaking away from his real wife and kids, the ones who got to share his last name and smile at his side in Christmas-card photos, Pop climbed onto the roof. Sometimes he allowed me to follow him. He drank beer and spit pistachio shells over the eaves and let me sip from his cans, sharp-mouthed things that bent under the pressure of my teeth and sliced shallow, stinging cuts into my tongue.

He told me stories about the constellations, but they were the wrong stories, ones that gave me nightmares. Orion, he said, was a space monster who skewered the skulls of his three greatest kills onto his belt so the rest of the universe would fear him. Not the kind of story a grown man should tell a kid or one you'd think a university professor would tell at all. Still, when I look up and see those three dots in a row, I know my father is out there somewhere, lying to another little schmuck who idolizes him, and I feel better.

But I didn't get to see the belt or any other part of Orion that night, not even his bloody armpit or that bright spot in his foot. The whole constellation was gone. And it wasn't even cloudy. Lots of other stars were out. I'm no astronomer, but even I can make out the dippers, some of the zodiac signs, that woman in the upside-down chair, and the one with the Dog Star in it. But no Orion.

I looked through the window. Serena wasn't in the bedroom, but I wasn't sure if she'd left, so I decided to take a walk. I crawled backward off the roof to the fire escape fast and rough and loud, slamming my elbows and toes and knees wherever I could. When I slid over the edge onto the iron ladder, a piece of gutter came down with me. It pinballed between my building and the next. When it hit the ground, it made a noise like a car wreck. *Great,* I thought. *Now the landlord is going to give me shit.*

Some of the other tenants poked their heads out of their windows, but when they saw it was just me, they rolled their eyes or sucked their teeth and ducked back inside to read or watch TV or do whatever it is other insomniacs do. Someone threw a half-full, plastic soda bottle at me. It landed at my feet. I uncapped it and threw it back, listening to the *splat, splat, splat* of it painting everything in sugar.

On the ground, I thought about looking for the clock, but decided not to. It was there somewhere and always would be so long as I didn't check. After a few, unsuccessful, cool-down loops around the block, I went inside and punched things—the couch cushions, the bedroom pillows, the beanbag in the corner of the living room—glad that Serena had decided to take off without confronting me.

~~~

The next day was Wednesday and felt like it. Just as much space and time still ahead of you as behind; no wonder people are always offing themselves on Wednesdays. Walking down the stairs, I could hear the landlord shuffling papers in his office. Unless I wanted to sneak down the fire escape again, which I did not, I had to pass him on my way out. His door was open and when he saw me, he rubbed a palm across his wrinkled forehead and sighed, which was worse than giving me shit. When my mother used to say, *Carlos's gotten into another fight* or *His grades keep slipping* or *Please, help me out here,* my father used to sigh over me, too, like he was saying, *Well, what can you expect?*

The front door made a noise like a shutter slamming against a house in a hurricane when it latched into place, and still I heard the landlord's second sigh, loud and obnoxious, as I shut it.

~~~

At work, I sorted mail on reflex, dropping each piece into its corresponding slot like you recall your phone number or five times five is twenty-five or ROYGBIV: without having to think about it.

It's funny the things I know about the people on my route when they don't know a thing about me. For instance, Eleanor Johnson (wife of Martin, sometimes addressed as Marty), 1725 Elm Street, has a birthday coming up. Starting in a couple of days and continuing for about a week, she will receive between seven and twelve birthday cards, most of which come from other Johnsons with return addresses in Tennessee.

One guy is obsessed with power tools. Every week he gets a new tool magazine. His name is Arthur, and no one calls him "Art," not if they know what's good for them. I once handed him a letter addressed to Art Walsh, 33 Newton Street. He dropped it onto his cement steps, pulled a pack of matches out of his overalls, lit one, and dropped that, too.

He said to me, "You ever see another letter from that fucker, throw it right in the trash." He slammed his door, leaving the letter flaming on his front step. I left it, too. I had a schedule to keep, and I was already running behind, like usual. You wouldn't believe how much time you can waste doing things like stepping on steps, walking up walkways, opening and closing mailboxes, and watching people set things on fire.

Oh, and there's Faye. I like Faye. 1187 Crescent Lane, smoking hot and fickle, she paints her front door a different color every three months and owns a Victoria's Secret worth of lingerie, if her packages are anything to go by. I like to play birthday with her padded envelopes, shifting them from hand to hand, shaking them, and imagining the size, shape, and color of the fabric inside.

It's strange to think of these people and their attachments to the world and me the invisible thread between, like dark matter stretched between stars. What would happen if I ran off with their mail? Or if I threw it all away? Would they become untethered, isolated little sparks in the sky, like Orion without his foot? Or would they find other ways to hang together? Serena would say there's always a way, if you really want it, and if you try hard enough. But what does she know about it?

I was pulling down mail, securing each route with a rubber band and tossing it into its tray, almost home free, when my boss showed up. He strolled across the mail room, smiling that stupid, sunny smile at everyone, but he was headed straight for me.

"Good morning, Carlos."

"Yeah, hello."

"Are you feeling alright? You look sort of, um, peeved. Well," he paused to adjust his glasses and chuckled, a stupid rumble that went on too long, "more than usual."

"Yeah, yeah. I'm peachy. Just heading out." I lifted the tray onto my hip.

"Well, alright. If you say so."

"I do."

"Well. Let me know if you need anything."

"Sure."

"And, Carlos? Try to remember to tuck in your shirt today." And then he smiled again, like it was all a joke, that head-turning, gossip-milling, probably-should-have-lost-me-my-job argument we had right here just yesterday in which I'd exploded, and he'd taken it all like a saint.

"Right." I headed out to pack my truck with other people's coupons and credit-card offers and letters from family and friends that they take for granted when I'd wrestle a cougar for the chance to send my father a piece of junk in the mail.

I did not tuck in my shirt.

~~~

I don't know why I was so sure, but all day I kept waiting to hear something about Orion. I kept an earbud in, flipping through news podcasts with one hand. I could walk my route in my sleep, and that day, I walked it without looking, my eyes glued to my phone, checking one news site after the other. But there was nothing.

At the end of my shift, I parked the truck, dropped off the dead mail, turned in my key, and decided to foot it home.

It was cold, the kind of dead-of-winter, single-digit cold I remembered from my childhood. I wondered if this was how space felt: this stinging, biting pain. But of course not. Space would be so much colder and so much quieter. There wouldn't be all this noise and hustle. Teenagers bundled in their bubble coats, smacking their lips together beneath the glass shelters of bus stops, bodies desperate for each other. Tires squealing to stops and starts, fleeing and seeking the company of other human beings. Department of Public Works staffers in their hunter orange stripes jackhammering away cement chunks, doing their jobs.

I walked through all this mundaneness, all this typical humanity, all these people with their connections to others, and tried not to be pissed off by its ugliness. Even the sunset, which should have been beautiful, its hue a vulnerable pinkish red, like the flesh beneath a nail when you press on it and the blood rushes to the surface, was deformed by the smog pumping from the smokestacks of the oil refinery and the phony light diffused from street lamps, porches, and office buildings.

THE THING WITH THE STARS | 37

All the while, the cold snapped at my eyes and nose and ears. I didn't mind. I was always so, so hot, like there was a nuclear reactor inside me, spitting out heat non-stop.

I wasn't walking home. I wasn't even walking in the right direction. I didn't know where I was going until I was there, at the weird store downtown with the huge, grimy glass windows and no sign on the door. No hours, no name. As usual, it was so dim it was hard to tell if the place was open or closed. I squinted, but I couldn't see who was at the counter. There was usually an old lump of a person there, maybe a man, maybe a woman.

I did see the shapes of globes in a back corner, though, and I figured, hey, why not? I went inside. A little bell sounded above my head, a warped, wrong sound, like *dwang*. At the counter, there was a girl with blue hair. She looked up at the sound of the bell, but didn't say anything, so neither did I.

I cut a sharp right, into the closest aisle. The store was strange. Random items were stacked in Jenga-like piles, ready to tip at the slightest nudge. I passed what looked like a bunch of handmade brooms, straw bristles twined around rough wood. A heap of porcelain dolls with skewed limbs stared glassily as I walked by. There was one of those machines you see in planetariums, a star projector, in one corner, casting strange shapes around the store, more like a disco ball than a piece of science equipment.

In the Earth and space section, there was a pile of globes, most of them peeling and out of date. I spun one. A smattering of browned, extinct countries twirled by: Zaire, Ceylon, Yugoslavia. On the shelves were maps, atlases, compasses, miniature helms, and bottled boats. On the floor, telescopes notched together like a haphazard Lincoln Log cabin. Some were wood, some were plastic, and some were metal. Some were tripods and some were handheld. Nothing in the aisle seemed to have been made after the year 1970.

I grabbed a star map that looked like someone had printed it from the Internet in black and white and then laminated it. It had the degrees of latitude and longitude and the winter constellations, though. I could use it. Just to check. It wasn't like I thought there was really anything to worry about. I just wanted to make sure I was looking in the right place the next time I was drunk and pitching a fit to keep myself from coming up with crackpot, non-sense theories like the stars were dropping out of the sky.

At the counter, the girl rung up my items. She put them in a hemp bag. She took my money. She gave me change. She handed over the bag. All silently. All while looking right through me, without the slightest bit of interest.

"What happened to the man who used to work here?" I asked.

The girl's focus sharpened. "Honestly? He's dead. Did you know him?"

"No, I just saw him sometimes."

"Lucky you."

I bit the inside of my cheek until I tasted blood and left. Lucky me. Fuck her. When I said I didn't know if it was a man or a woman who worked here? I lied. It was a man. I always thought he looked a bit like Pop. He slicked his hair back the same way, and had these stupid glasses, and this dumb off-centeredness to his mouth. And his eyes were brown. The blue-haired girl's eyes were brown, too. Maybe she was my long-lost sister. Maybe I should have asked her, *Did he give you nightmares about the stars, too? Have you noticed anything weird about the night sky since he died?* But that was nonsense because Pop wasn't dead. I would have known if he were.

~~~

At home, the light on the answering machine flashed. I tossed my coat onto the nearest piece of furniture and ignored the twinkling red light. It would only be Serena, and I wasn't ready to talk to her yet. I could only say things that would push her away forever. Like one object tipped off a tower slightly later than another; I'd never be able to make up the arm's distance to reach her.

Instead, I headed to the roof. The walk home had taken a while and it was well past dark. I looked for Orion again, trying to convince myself I was just being a dumb shit, but I still couldn't see it.

I tried from the opposite direction. I faced north, toward the city, and looked for the dippers. They were there, all fourteen stars visible, if dim, bears or plows or wagons or gourds or walls or coffins or whatever they're supposed to be. Pop said they were meat cleavers, spinning through the sky, flying toward their mark. Whatever they are, they were there.

THE THING WITH THE STARS | 39

I unrolled the star map. It was hard to see the dark map in the dim light cast by the streetlights, but I didn't feel like going back inside for a flashlight. Draco's tail was supposed to curl between the dippers. I looked up. It was there, too.

Draco, there's a constellation that looks like its stories. No need for Pop to exaggerate. It did look like a dragon, or a snake anyway, twisting around the dippers. I could easily make out some of the bright stars in its head, snapping toward Hercules.

Also in their places were Cepheus, the king, Cassiopeia, the vain and upside-down wife, Andromeda, the damsel in distress, Cetus, the monster, and Perseus, the savior. To me they looked like a pentagon, a lightning bolt, a sharp-nailed finger, a coat hanger, and a stethoscope. Still though, nice to have your whole story up in the sky, remembered forever. Who will remember me or Mom, the ghost family? We hardly exist. Whatever they looked like, the northern stars were all in their places. But in the south, things got weird.

It was a wasteland. No matter how many times I looked down at my map and then back up into the sky, there was nothing. No Canis Major, no omega-shaped Gemini, no Orion, no Taurus, like those y-shaped sticks people use to find water. And fine, I couldn't find the constellations. That wasn't a big deal. I knew it wasn't. Light pollution alone could account for that. Like most people, I lived in a place with those ugly light poles every thirty-five feet, like one-legged metal giraffes. But I couldn't even find the brightest stars: Sirius, the orange-ish head of the brighter twin, Orion's red armpit or blue foot, or the red eye of the bull. It was like there was a boundary in the sky, like the edges of a black hole, and everything that fell below it got crushed or eaten or erased. Which was crazy. But I felt it anyway.

Irritated, I flopped onto the roof. It made a racket, and the gritty tar paper scratched my bare elbows and calves. It was cold, but that was fine. More than. I wanted it cold. I needed it cold to bank the fiery roiling in my core.

In the pocket of my jeans, my cell phone vibrated, but I let it be. If I answered it, things would go sour fast. But if I let the call go to voicemail, then there would always be a message waiting for me. No matter how far away I drifted from this moment and this place, someone, somewhere (not someone, of course, but Serena) once sent words for me, like a beam of light or a radio wave shot into space, hopeful of finding themselves not alone, and reached me, eventually, whether they knew it or not.

~~~

I woke up late in the center of the roof, nose clogged, head pounding, and eye lashes frosted shut. I stretched my stiff fingers, rubbed my face, and then stumbled through the window to take a quick, hot shower and drink a cup of coffee before heading to work.

The door to the landlord's office was open. As I walked past it, I saw him rub his crinkled, paper bag fingers against his temples, but I had no time to be pissed about it.

I had to skip a few lights, but I managed to make it to the post office on time. At work, I sorted mail haphazardly, snapping my fingers in the rubber bands I rolled over my route bundles. My boss looked me up and down, his gaze like search beams, assessing. He opened his pocked, crusted lips to criticize, but then his eyes snagged on mine, and he crushed his lips together and kept his mouth shut. Good.

On my route, I was a mess. The first sign was at the Dominics' place. I pushed my fingers through the mail slot, and their Doberman nipped my fingers. The rookiest of rookie mistakes. At Faye's purple door, I got to the bottom of the steps and wasn't sure whether I was supposed to turn left or right for the next house. By ten-thirty I'd used both of my ten-minute breaks, and I'd spent them in the truck with my forehead pressed to the steering wheel, knees bouncing, hands twitching, cheeks burning with anger I couldn't direct at anybody.

The stars are falling out of the sky. The stars are falling out of the sky. The stars are falling out of the sky.

It was dumb as dirt, but I felt it, and every time I thought it, my heart wobbled like a planet passing in front of a star. I didn't scan my barcode items because I was so behind schedule sending no data to the post office seemed no worse than transmitting my actual location. When my stomach started to rumble around noon, I rooted in my pockets and under the seat, but there was nothing to eat. No candy bars or even gum. I'd been running too late this morning to think of lunch, of course.

I drove to a gas station. Inside, I bought a saran-wrapped roast beef sandwich, a Mars bar, and a bottle of Coke.

The man at the register was middle-aged and dark-haired, with the disapproving frown of a father. He bagged my items slowly.

"Never seen you here before," he said.

"No," I agreed, hand clenching around the buzzing phone in my pocket. It might have been Serena. But then, it might also have been work, wondering where the hell I was and why I hadn't checked in.

"You supposed to drive that thing here?" he asked, head tilted at the truck visible outside the greasy, floor-to-ceiling glass wall all gas stations seem to have, the one that lets the attendants spy on people that might be trying to steal gas. "My brother-in-law drives one. Says they're pretty strict 'bout that sort of thing."

"Sure. It's on my route."

He handed over my change and the plastic bag full of my items, sealed and capped, like space food. "Right."

I took the bag.

In the truck, I chewed slowly, trying not to think what I was thinking: that Pop would know what was up with the stars, that it would be easy enough to find him. One Google search, and *bam*, I'd have a number or an address or a place of work.

I took out my phone and stared at it. There were thin cracks in the screen, gossamer as gas floating between solar systems, from months ago when I'd launched it at Serena. Well, not at Serena. At the door after she'd walked out.

I couldn't look him up. When you seek, you find. When you scour the universe for intelligent life, eventually you find creatures smarter and better and more evolved than you who see you as an ant sitting atop a nice pile of resources. If I looked him up, I'd know the truth. I'd know that he was still happily married and uninterested, or divorced and uninterested, or unlisted, or dead, like Mom. I put my phone away.

~~~

That night Perseus and his whole crew were gone. I went inside and sat on the couch, watching the news, first the six o'clock, and then the ten o'clock, and then whatever I could find. I kept expecting someone to say something about the stars. It wasn't a one-time thing, and it wasn't subtle. The sky was as dark and empty as the other side of the Moon, and the only reason anyone could see anything was the streetlights. Was it really possible that no one else had noticed?

But no one said anything. Either I was crazy, or they were covering it up. Which is exactly what they would do, wouldn't they, if there was a problem like this, a problem with the universe that they couldn't explain or predict or fix? I fell asleep on the couch, sweating and shaking, palms pressed to my chest.

~~~

I woke with a crick in my neck, heart pounding. I'd had a dream. In the dream I'd been floating in space, no suit, no oxygen, just checking out the stars, twinkling little pinpoints in the distance. I'd swiped my fingers back and forth, connecting them into shapes: Serena, my mom. Pop. Me. But then a wave of darkness crested over my constellations, darker than the darkness of space. I knew that wave was it: annihilation, the end of life and time, of the universe and everything in it.

I pushed myself off the couch and into the bathroom. It was still dark outside, and I splashed water on my face, trying to calm my trembling limbs. It hadn't been a nightmare. I wasn't afraid. Just annoyed. This was all Pop's fault with his dumbass stories.

~~~

Despite the dream, things weren't that bad at first. I downloaded an astronomy app on my phone. When I held the screen to different quadrants of the sky, it showed the locations of the stars with lines between them to make it easy to pick out the constellations. According to it, there was no problem. All the stars were in their proper places. So, for a while, I felt better. Reassured. I was just being nutso.

But then I realized the app was just a program running an algorithm to spit out the representations of the stars that *should* be up in the northern hemisphere in winter. And it was daylight besides. It was all hypothetical. My phone couldn't actually see the stars, didn't actually know anything. After that, I had to sit in the truck for a bit with my head between my knees.

On my route, I dragged my feet, hoping to run into someone on their way in or out of their door. I needed to speak to a human. I needed to hear someone say they'd noticed something, too. That even if we were all dying, at least I wasn't crazy. But it was hard. You'd be surprised how many people work nine-to-five. At Arthur's I gave up on serendipity and knocked.

"What?" he asked around a piece of half-chewed toast. "You need me to sign something?"

"Uh, no," I said, handing over his mail, a McMaster-Carr magazine and a couple of bills.

"Then what?" he asked, curling the sheaf into his back pocket. "I'm running late."

"Never mind. It's nothing, man. Go back to your day."

"Nah." He adjusted his worn belt and tucked his flannel. "You got me now. What d'ya want?"

"You notice anything weird with the stars lately?"

"How d'you mean, weird?"

I shifted my mailbag. It felt stupid, saying it out loud. "Like, missing. Not there. Any that you expected to see, but didn't?"

"I don't pay particular attention to the stars, to be honest with you."

"Yeah, but have you noticed it's darker at night? Anything like that?"

Arthur looked past me, rubbing a hand across his stubbled chin and throat. "You messing with me?"

"No. Forget it. Forget I said anything. You have a nice day."

"Yeah, alright," said Arthur, who was running late, but whose eyes I felt on my back all the way up the block. Inside, the magma churned, and I moved quick as I could out of Arthur's sight before I could convince myself to turn around and show him what was what.

That's when I decided enough was enough. I was quitting. I'd do it that night. I'd take the truck with me, just take off with all the undelivered packages, and give everyone a taste of what was to come, of what it felt like to be cut off from all their messages big and small, like we all would be soon from the warmth and light of the stars.

Maybe I'd even try to find Pop. Maybe he could explain what was happening, whatever small consolation understanding would be. I remembered the crest of darkness from my dream that morning, and I had to go sit in the truck for a while again.

~~~

I finished out my shift and delivered all the mail. Let them have one more day. But I didn't go back to the post office. I drove past it and kept driving. I stuck to the backroads, hoping to be ignored. I wasn't sure what would happen when I didn't turn in my truck.

The sky reddened, then dimmed, but windows and streetlamps glowed in the darkness, their light bouncing off the whiteness of the truck. It was so bright that for a while I thought about turning around. I thought again, *I must be crazy*. But as the houses thinned and the streetlamps stopped popping up so regularly at my sides, the darkness closed in. My headlights cut through the inky, heavy blackness, like a submarine's weak beams slicing through the depths of the ocean. I kept expecting to see a translucent eye scuttle by the windshield. But there was nothing. My phone buzzed and rattled against my thigh, a tiny rocket ship trying to take flight.

I drove for hours. I drove until I ran out of road at the bottom of a hill. When I pulled the key out of the ignition, it was so dark I couldn't see the hands in front of my face. I sat behind the wheel, breathing in and breathing out until I felt my legs could sustain me. Then I tumbled out of the truck onto the grass.

It was cold. Little, icy crystals clung to the blades beneath my palms. I tried to feel my old, perpetual heat, but I wasn't angry, only afraid. I didn't feel like the inside of a volcano, magma rolling inside; I felt like a frozen sea, icy waves sloshing beneath. I was too afraid to lift my head.

I climbed the hill on my hands and knees, head down, squinting at the ground. At the top of the hill, I rolled onto my back and squeezed my eyes shut. Here, on this buildingless, lightless hill, hours from the city, I should be able to see the stars. I should be able to see the whole Milky Way spilling across the sky, a perpetual, beautiful accident. If not here, then nowhere.

If I opened my eyes and the stars were there, then I would go home. I'd turn in my truck and face the music from my boss. I'd apologize to my landlord and pay for the gutter I knocked down.

I'd go downtown and ask the blue-haired girl at the store about the old man. I'd call Serena and agree to her demands: marriage, counseling, whatever. Maybe I'd even try to find Pop. Or go lay a bouquet on Mom's grave.

But if I opened my eyes at the stars were not there . . .

I thought of my dream, of the crest of oblivion bearing down on me. The ice ocean churned in my gut, and my jugular thumped hard beneath the flesh of my throat.

I opened my eyes.

The Child Breathes

When I wake, the child is cold and blue tinged. I didn't mean to sleep. I shouldn't have slept. Not once have I closed my eyes since the creature first appeared, wispy and spectral, at the edges of my vision three days ago, but it seems I have reached the point where even draughts and spells cannot keep the exhaustion at bay.

I place a palm on the child's chest. The echo of movement reverberates against her rib cage, so I call to the earth and demand its heat. I reach for the sky and pull its wind, its spark. I pray it is enough.

Horance bolts upright in bed, rubbing his ears as the child takes a shallow, rattling breath.

He tumbles to his knees beside the rocking chair. "Gods! Is she . . . ?"

"Put on your armor," I say, not looking at him, focusing my magic into our daughter, looking for color, for movement, hoping for more little expansions of chest.

"But the babe," he says. "I want to be here when, if . . ."

"I will take care of the babe," I say.

He touches my shoulder, gently fingering the frizzled braid hanging there.

"You cannot keep this up," he says. "Perhaps it is time . . ."

"Don't forget your sword. The one I enchanted with earth magic. None other."

Horance dips his head and leaves.

I can't worry after him. We have a plan this time.

~~~

When the babe has stabilized enough for my satisfaction, I lay her against my chest and wind a long cloth around her. I cinch the fabric at my waist and depart empty-handed, trusting my body and my magic to provide.

Outside, the sun crests the horizon. Clouds spill like blood across the pale flesh of the sky. The rosy light drenches Horance, who stands in the center of the courtyard in full chainmail, the charmed great sword gleaming aloft before him. His knuckles, blanched as bone, clench the hilt. Hilda perches on the rooftop opposite, footing sure against the loose slate tiles.

"Is it here?" Horance asks.

I nod. Behind him, the creature shimmers.

"Where?" He spins. His sword slashes through the air the creature appears to inhabit. Hilda draws her bow and swivels, following my gaze, but it's obvious she also can't see it. Horance thinks me mad with grief, I know, but Hilda holds her bow taut and keeps her eyes on me, completely trusting.

How odd to think this girl, this strange, mute and sullen girl we stumbled into taking in, might be the closest thing to a child I will ever have.

No. I won't let that be. I cannot move the creature. I cannot force her fully into this realm. But if I can see her, if she can stretch her skeletal fingers out and touch my child, her realm and mine must overlap. I only must make them see her. What must I command? The earth to cling to her feet? The air to hold fast to her body?

Exhaustion pounds beneath my temples, but the child breathes, hot and moist against my throat, and I must keep it that way. I grip the iron banister that rails the balcony. It is wet and cold, covered in morning dew. I curl my fingers around the metal and project my will into the water that saturates the air, bidding the element to do as I command.

Hilda looses an arrow before I'm sure I've done anything. It pins the lower edge of the creature's damp robe to the ground. Horance follows with a swipe of his blade. The creature dodges and pulls itself free with a nonchalant tug.

I am supposed to flee, but I linger, as still and heavy as stone. I have more to lose than just the babe, I realize. And I have endangered them.

"Go!" Horance shouts. I release my grip on the rail. We have a plan, and I must follow it.

~~~

In the stable, I pet the trotter on the nose, once, quickly, before saddling her. I wish I could explain my haste, but I have no gift for communing with animals. I can only dig my heels into her flank and hope she senses my urgency.

As we gallop through the forest that rings the keep, the child is silent, lulled, perhaps, by the rocking of the horse.

We don't get far. I've only just begun to smell the salt and muck of the sea when a dark approximation of a stallion materializes alongside us. My horse, dear Lena, takes fright and veers off the path. I curl around the babe as branches slap my arms and cheeks.

We speed and slow, following Lena's confusion and fear. The stallion keeps pace. Its semiformed hooves don't bother to touch the ground. It is as fast as it needs to be, regardless of the shape or size of its legs, heedless of the smoothness or roughness of the path beneath its feet.

The horse's rider has garbed herself as a washed-out, colorless version of me. Her skin is as pale as the dusty moon. Her dress is a rotting rag that clings to her like seaweed on a corpse drowned days past. But she is me. The same shape of face. The same proportion of waist to hips. The same noose of a braid hanging over her shoulder.

"What have you done to Horance and Hilda?" I shout.

The creature rotates her head too far around. She looks at me with eyes wholly black and glistening, like a crow's, but her lips issue no message.

"Are they alive?"

Thrice I have met her, and she has never, not once, said a word. This time is no different. She holds my eyes, silent, while the horses gallop on in parallel. Did I think, truly, I could outrun her?

"Why?" I ask. "Why don't you leave us alone?" I lay my cheek against the babe's too-cold head. "Please."

The black stallion pulls ahead and turns sideways before us. Lena rears, careless of me and the babe. I grip her mane and beg the earth to pull her hooves to the ground. Somewhere a loon warbles its eerie wail.

The creature draws an arm through the air, and it parts like a curtain, revealing behind it a shambling horde of men, women, and children. They are shadows, wraiths. They are the dead. I do not want to look too closely, but I cannot help seeing. On the ground, a tot's whole face lights up as she smiles silently at me, having died too young to learn to say "hello" or "mama."

I pull a weak bolt of lightning from the sky, more flash than heat. The creature's horse steps primly aside, but the arm drops, and the portal snaps shut. I slump forward against Lena's neck. Her coarse hair scratches my face. The babe's whuffs of breath come so far apart.

"Take me, too," I·say, wetting Lena's mane. "Please."

The creature seizes Lena's reins. Lena stamps and snorts.

I pat her neck. "Go on," I say, and she does.

~~~

The creature reverses our trip, back through the forest and into the stable. I dismount, so weak I barely land on my feet. In the courtyard, arrows and blood splinter and speckle the soil, but there is no sign of Horance or Hilda. I stumble through the halls of my home, not looking at the paintings hanging on the walls, bitter reminders of the children that were and are not.

I find Horance and Hilda in the closet that we turned into Hilda's room. The girl's pointed chin rests atop the sheets, almost as ashen as the linens. Horance sits on a stool beside the bed. He has stripped to the waist and wound a bandage sloppily around his ribs.

I kneel beside him and place my head in his lap. He brushes the wetness from my face with gentle fingertips. "Is she . . .?"

Please, I beseech the sky and the earth, the ocean and the air. I feel them touch me, little swipes of sympathy, clumsy as the hands of infants. But life and death are not within their power or mine.

"No," I say. "But soon."

I unwrap the babe and lay her in Horance's arms. He rocks her and hums a lullaby. I pull myself into the bed alongside Hilda. I place a palm on her chest. Her lungs expand. Her heart beats. Whatever damage she suffered in the courtyard, she brims still with warmth and life.

The creature stands in the corner of the room, dark, and silent, and patient. I close my eyes, unhook my magic from the babe, and let exhaustion take me under.

Are You Even Alive in There?

I'm only writing this stupid thing because my psychiatrist says I should. And I'm only listening to him because of the thing that happened with Jan on Christmas.

If I were the sort of person to have a best friend, Jan would be it. Which is sad, really, because to Jan I'm nobody. Just some artsy loser she ran into same time, same place every week during college: in the cafeteria, at dinnertime, reaching for the same slice of chocolate cake. The first week, she jumped back like a scalded cat, fluttered her big, blue eyes, and said, *Oh! I'm sorry!* The next time, she carefully extended her pink-polished nails and murmured, *Pardon me.* The time after that, she flipped all that sandy hair over her shoulder and simpered, *Fancy meeting you here.*

Eventually she noticed a photo sticking out of the planner balanced on the edge of my tacky, orange tray. It was something dumb, like a frat boy tossing a Frisbee, but she smiled so her dimples showed. *Where did you get that?* she asked. When I told her I took it, she gushed for so long I had to follow her to a table and drop down into the seat across from her.

After that, we often ate together, in the back corner of the cafeteria, where the gray, pinwheel-patterned linoleum tiles were most dingy, me rocking dry, spongy chocolate across my tongue, trying and failing to experience the bliss that shimmered across Jan's face every time she slid a bite between her painted lips, and Jan looking laser-beam straight into my eyes and talking about the value of art and the sorts of things I could do with it to make money.

And sure, that sounds nice. Like we were all chummy. But I saw Jan sometimes when she didn't see me. I saw the way she was pals with everyone. If some awkward, fumbling girl with a pocket protector and braces bumped into her at lunch, Jan would end up taking her to a party that night. She'd go into the school store to buy a pencil and get to talking so long with the stupid jock cashier she'd end up walking him home after his shift was over, then tutoring him all semester. That's just the way Jan was. Still is. I'm just another wet, abandoned puppy squatting under the eaves of an all-night diner that she can't ignore. But still, she makes an effort to keep in contact, and that's nice of her.

So, Jan came over on Christmas. I could tell she meant it to be brief, a quick stop between one place and the next just to say, *Merry Christmas.* When I heard her knock—a rhythmic, assertive one, two, three—I was lounging on the couch in pajamas, the fleecy, fern green ones my mom bought me years ago, maybe the last thing she ever bought me before she died, drinking eggnog out of a mug and watching *A Charlie Brown Christmas.*

I opened the door. Jan was wearing a Santa Claus hat—the fuzzy, white ball at the tip dangled over one pearl-studded ear—and a frozen, staged smile, like the ones people flash as they count down to cheese right before a camera shutter clicks. The smile drooped fast, and the lines at the corners of her mouth dipped into downward curlicues as she took in my attire.

She said, *I thought you were going to try to have some family over this year.* I said, *I was.* And then she said, *Well, what happened?* And I said, *Same thing that happens every year. It didn't work out.* She sighed, a gust of breath like the kickup before a tiny storm and whispered, *Oh, Isabelle.* I told her, *It's fine. I'm not into holidays anyway,* but still she stepped over the threshold, black pumps thumping across my cheap, laminate floor, and walked into the kitchen.

I didn't follow her. Instead, I flexed my stiff toes, trying to coax some warmth into them. Futile; I'm almost always cold. When Jan reappeared, she held a champagne flute of eggnog and looked like a woman returning from powdering her nose: her cheeks were rosier, her lipstick glossier, her eyes brighter; she had put herself together.

We sat on the couch and she told me a bunch of things I only vaguely remember. Something about a product jingle she was working on. For a vacuum cleaner? Something about a new boyfriend. Something about ham dinner with her mother and ice-skating with her nieces and nephews. The details didn't interest me. I watched her wool sweater shift across her shoulder blades as she talked and soaked up the steady, soothing kindness flowing through her voice.

After a while, she stood and wandered through my apartment. I found her in the usual spot, in my office, crouched, sifting through the piles of photographs littering the floor. Jan liked the Christmassy ones: three story homes crisscrossed with blinking lights; plastic reindeer grazing on lawns; fake Kris Kringles sitting on wooden thrones, bouncing squirming snowsuit-clad toddlers on their knees; things like that. My favorites were the accidents, the happenstances, the flashes of emotion that lasted only moments in life, but would linger, ghostly, within the glossy paper forever: the twist of a runner's lips as she trips over a curb into the street; the hunched shoulders of a homeless man as he watches commuters stream by with coffees and cannoli and meat-stuffed bagels; the blown pupils of two teenagers as they look at each across a café booth filled with their friends.

I don't understand why you never try to sell these, Jan said. *Or at least frame them.* I shrugged. It was hard to explain, to Jan or anyone else, that I didn't want to show off my work. Each picture contained a secret, stolen, voyeuristic moment that sent a rare wave of warmth and shame rolling through my abdomen, like guzzling a glass of hot cocoa on a cold day while a stranger freezes to death on the porch. Pinning them to walls would be like pulling off my clothes and masturbating in the center of a four-lane highway. Jan looked longingly at a few of the photos. I knew she wanted to ask if she could take some, no doubt to talk them up to people who could turn me into the sort of hot shot who wouldn't have to spend Christmas alone, but we've had that conversation ad nauseum, so she just caressed their edges, then replaced them.

On her way out, Jan gave me a hug. Her hair tickled my nose, the mounds of her breasts squashed mine, and the scent of her perfume—a thick, sweet, syrupy smell, like canned peaches—clung to my sweater all night. In a voice that prodded with gentle, apologetic fingertips, she said, *It's not right, you know, living like this. Maybe you should think about getting some help.* And then she left.

I'd heard this kind of thing before. The pastor, at my mother's funeral had said, *It's okay if you cry. You don't have to hold back.* Whenever I invite my sister to visit, she says, *I can't. We're spending the holiday with Jacob's family, but you should spend it with some friends.* In college, my dorm mates cajoled, *Come on! You can't stay in every weekend.* Once, when I orgasmed quietly and without fanfare, as per usual, one of my dull, monogamous boyfriends said, *Jeez are you even alive in there?* So I figured maybe they had a point, and called a psychiatrist.

~~~

I don't talk to Doctor Seever much. His office is distracting. I spend the hour trying to decipher the logic in the calligraphed kanji numerals on the face of the clock. Or I stare at the fountain in the eastern corner, a five-foot-tall slab of stained glass, wondering how the liquid trickles back to the top. Or I gaze at the room's mahogany paneling, uncovering stories in the rings and knots. There, a man hanging from a noose. There, a tortoise. There, an angel or, maybe, a crow.

Or I sneak glances at Dr. Seever. His thick, circular glasses. The shaving bumps that line the tan skin of his throat. His pinstripe shirts. The small sliver of hairy ankle exposed when he crosses one leg over the other. The way he twirls his pen between the index and middle fingers of one hand but holds the other perfectly still on the arm of his chair. I try not to feel any forbidden, little thrills. I listen to his watch ticking, anticipating, muscles increasingly tense, the passing of the last second of our session. And every time I stand to leave, I think, *Oh, no. That's it.* Today Doctor Seever said, *It's your choice to come here, Isabelle. No one is forcing you.* I said, *I know.* Then he said, *Well, will you share anything with me today?* And I said, *No.*

He was disappointed. He huffed, an exasperated little sound in the back of his throat that I don't think I was supposed to hear. It reminded me of the noise my mom used to make when I'd sit at the kitchen table doing homework and she'd stand at the stove, wearing some absurdly bright dress, like neon green, electric yellow, sunburst orange, or robin's egg blue, with her long, dark hair swinging in a loose braid down her back, doing what seemed like a million things at once—boiling pasta in a deep metal pot, frying sweet Italian sausage in a skillet, rubbing spices into chicken or beef to cook later, and chopping vegetables for salad—and I'd say, *Mom, what's negative three square root three k plus four times the square root of three k minus five?* and she'd say, without even turning around, *I don't know, baby, why don't you ask your sister?*

I'd make a face. And then Mom would make the sound, that frustrated, underbreath huff and say, *Honestly, what is wrong with you two?* Then she'd raise her voice and call, *Elena, Elena.* And Elena would stride into the kitchen, pants impeccably pressed, button-down, collared shirt heavily starched, and hair swept back into a bun so tight it stretched her eyes thin and narrow. *Yes, Mother?* she'd say. And then Mom would say, *Help your sister with her homework, please.* And Elena would suck her teeth and roll her eyes and tell me the answers without explaining anything and stomp upstairs to her room. Then Mom would make the sound again and say, *What a pair you two are.*

So when Doctor Seever made the sound, I felt guilty. I said, *I went to CVS today. They already had Valentine's Day decorations.* He said, *OK. Did that bother you?* I shrugged.

They did bother me. I hated the little kisses wrapped in their cold, crinkly foil, the heart-boxed chocolates, the plush, fuzzy bears that jiggled and sang, the powdery candy hearts declaring their love in shorthand, and the fake roses with their stiff, lipstick-red, polyester petals and their Crayola-green stems and their harmless, plastic thorns, signifying passion and embodying none.

I didn't linger. I picked up my glossy printer paper and a quart of milk and checked out. The woman behind the cash register wore colorful gem rings on the fingers of her right hand—emeralds, rubies, diamonds, sapphires, and opals, too dull, too translucent to be real.

I didn't make small talk with her the way people usually do with cashiers. I didn't say, *So how're things going around here? Must be busy lately, huh? All this Valentine's Day crap must get annoying to shelve. How do you get the glitter off?* Or even, *Have a nice day.* When she handed over my bag, our fingers touched. Her flesh against mine felt unreal, like plastic or wax. *Thank you,* I said.

When I got home, I called Elena. She didn't answer, but I didn't expect her to. I left a message asking her if she wanted to do something for Easter. It was still almost a month away, but the earlier the better with her. At the end of the message I said, perhaps, a bit, meanly, *Say hello to Jacob for me.*

~~~

I had lunch with Jan today. It was a nice break. I had a bad morning at the print shop. My boss yelled at me for fiddling with a poster design again. I wanted to make the client's sky-blue background a deeper, darker blue and the leaves on the plants winding around the edges of the poster more yellow-green than forest.

For a while I got away with changing the posters, because by the time anyone realized what I'd done, they were already printed and back to the clients, who didn't pay enough attention to complain, and I could claim it was an accident. But now my boss checks my designs carefully before they go to print. I usually have two ready, one exactly as the client specified and one with my own tweaks.

Today, he leaned over me, planting his meaty, pink palms on my desk so I could see the thick, dark hairs running up his forearms, squinted at my computer screen, then bared his yellow, coffee-stained teeth, rolled his steely, blue-gray, bloodshot eyes, and barked, *For fuck's sake, Isabelle, just give the clients what they ask for,* blowing putrid caffeine-cigarettes-tuna breath across my cheek. *Alright,* I said and did what I was told. As I tend to. Usually.

For lunch, Jan had a meatless, spinach salad. She ate it in dainty bites that never smudged her lipstick. I had a burger, and she scolded me for eating like a teenager, but her tone wasn't sharp. She was in a good mood. One of her legs crossed over the other, and her sheer stockings gleamed as she bounced her knee. She kept grinning, flashing her straight, white teeth, and rushing through sentences so fast she'd run out of breath in the middle and have to stop and gulp in some air to finish them.

Outside, snow slid slushily into the sewers just in time for people like Jan to enjoy Valentine's Day weekend. That's what she was going on about. The new boyfriend, Hugh, and how great he was. How he was picking her up from lunch so I could meet him. How they were going to spend the holiday at some romantic cabin in the woods. How she was going to bring him home to meet her family on Easter. I smiled and nodded and said, *That's great* in the appropriate places. If I wasn't as enthusiastic as friends are supposed to be about these things, Jan didn't mention it.

Hugh turned out to be built like a Renaissance statue. He was tall and thin and lightly muscled. His skin was the color of a walnut; his eyes were like molten amber. When Jan introduced us, he said, *So this is the artist, huh?* and gave me a look that, if it could, would have singed the collar of my sweater, sent tendrils of smoke crawling along each individual woven strand, caused smoldering tatters of ash to fall away from my skin, and left me bare. A knot of heat pulsed beneath my belly button. I wished I had my camera.

The look was masked in a moment, transformed into curious, artificial politeness. *It's good to finally meet you,* he said. *You should have dinner with us sometime. Jan and I love photography. I'd love to talk to you about it.*

I looked at Jan. Her lips were curved into a tight, hopeful smile. I wondered if I should warn Jan about Hugh, but I didn't know how. I said, *I'll think about it.* Hugh smiled, and Jan frowned, but I figured it was safer that way. I'm never a good choice for a third wheel on a date. Ask Elena. She still hasn't forgiven me.

On the way out, Jan pulled me aside in the vestibule. *What do you think?* she asked. She unwound my scarf and reknotted it the way she likes. Her eyes were wide, and the muscles in her neck and the parts of her shoulders I could see above the cut of her blouse were tense. *He seems like an alright guy,* I said and watched her clavicles drop, relaxed. *Good,* she said. *I'm glad.* And then, *Do me a favor and call up your sister, okay? You should spend time with her. She's the only family you've got. I don't like going away and leaving you alone.* I grabbed her long, thin fingers, which were pulling the scarf too tight around my neck, breathed in her warm, sweet perfume, and said, *Yes, Jan. You know I'll try.*

After work, I went for a walk in the park near my apartment. It's not much to look at. Just a few sapling oak trees, a handful of limestone benches, and a grimy jungle gym at the center, like an ancient papier-mâché spider. There was a young couple walking. Their joined hands swung between them, and sometimes their hips bumped. I thought I was in for some scripted, messy PDA— no one knows how to play the parts Valentine's Day dictates like teenagers—but that wasn't what happened.

They weren't just moving through a set of choreographed steps. Their eyes darted at each other, then away, then back. Their locked fingers twitched and rubbed and grasped, never holding still. Their smiles were wide and unwilting. Their cheeks were flushed with pleasure. I stuck my hand into my knapsack, rummaging for my camera. I knew they'd kiss soon, and I wanted to capture it, that moment right before connection when want flutters in the stomach and anticipation sears the spine. The moment right before you realize a kiss is just a kiss: wet, writhing tongue and shortness of breath and complete lack of fireworks behind the eyelids. I wanted to own that moment, to be able to pull it out later and stare at it and remember that passion exists, however transient. I snapped the picture just in time.

When I got home, there was a message from Elena on my answering machine. It was eight words long. It went, *Going to Jacob's parents' for Easter, as usual.*

~~~

Valentine's Day came, like a spill spreading across a watercolor, devastating and inevitable, then was gone. I had been sitting on the couch, wriggling the toes within my socks, Smartwool ones that Jan bought for Christmas, sipping cocoa, and watching one of the dozens of romantic comedies on TV, when someone knocked on the door—five breakneck, jerky raps. I hadn't been expecting anyone, so I padded across the floor, avoiding the creaky sections in case I felt like pretending I wasn't home. I closed one eye, pressed my palms against the splintery door, and looked through the peephole.

It was Hugh. He was wearing a black silk shirt and he was pacing. A single red rose dangled from the fingers of his right hand. I jerked back and stepped on a metal dustpan I'd forgotten to put away. It clattered under my heel. Hugh called my name as pain zinged through my foot, and I knew I was in trouble.

Everything turned oversensitive. My tongue against my teeth. The dry skin at my knees and elbows. Arousal bloomed between my hips. I wanted to let Hugh in, to kiss him, to feel his hands on my clavicles, against my abdomen, between my thighs. I wanted to take him to bed and hear him moan my name in that helpless, broken way men do when they climax.

It was Elena's first date all over again. She was seventeen, and I didn't see what the big deal was; I'd been dating boys quietly for years. But Elena announced it at breakfast like the Pope was coming to town. I remember I was eating a powdered doughnut.

Mother, she said, *I'm going out with John Davidson this weekend.* And Mom said, *Okay, but only if you take Isabelle with you.* I licked the sugar from my fingers while Elena debated and argued, then screamed and begged, knowing I was just as powerless to change Mom's mind.

So on Friday night, I went out with Elena and Johnny David, which is what everyone except my sister called him. Johnny wore leather jackets, smoked cigarettes, and had a head full of dark, curly hair. Emotions too hot to face sizzled through his irises. He was a dream. The first photo I ever took was of Johnny David shooting dice a block from school when he (and I) should have been in class. I'll never understand how Elena snagged a date with him. Maybe he considered her a challenge. Or just didn't believe she could be as uptight as she seemed.

For the date, Elena dragged us out to dinner at some stuffy restaurant with a menu full of foreign words and then to a romantic comedy. I split with Elena and Johnny at the theater so they could sit alone in the back, but I could tell by Johnny's face after that Elena hadn't let him touch so much as her big toe. So I said, *Let's have some fun.* Elena frowned, but Johnny smiled at me, crooked and sly, and said, *What do you have in mind?*

We ended up at a pool hall. I beat Johnny four games to three while Elena stood in a corner, pulling her pink cardigan tight across her chest and flinching at discarded beer bottles like she expected them to nip her shins. I suspect Johnny went easy on me toward the end, but I earned at least two of those wins.

Johnny walked us home. When we parted, he shook Elena's hand, because that's all she would let him do, but he kissed me on the cheek and said, *It was a pleasure, Isabelle.* Heat raced up my neck, and I hoped it didn't show. Inside, Elena pushed me into the coat rack so roughly I still have a scar from where one of the pegs dug into my shoulder blade. She said, *I hate you,* then ran upstairs before I could retaliate.

Down the hall, Mom's door squeaked open. Her long, dark hair spilled across the front of her white nightgown. She was beautiful in the dim, blue light. *What's the matter?* she asked. *You and Elena aren't fighting again, are you?* She looked so worried, I could only lie. *No*, I said. *Good*, she said. *It's about time you two learned to get along.* When I got to my room, Johnny was tapping on my window. When I opened it, it wasn't to spite my sister. It was because, when he looked at me, I felt ablaze.

Now, as Hugh called my name, I could feel the veins pounding beneath my skin. Even remembering Elena and Johnny and how I was wearing socks that Jan had bought me, I wanted to let him in. I hunkered in my office and stared at the pictures on the floor. I hunkered and hunkered. And looked and looked. And then I opened the door.

~~~

I have an appointment with Doctor Seever today. I don't know how to say the things I need to say. (That I am cold and numb except for when I'm not, and then I'm this out-of-control mess that hurts the people I love; and that even then, the heat is on the inside where no one can see it; and that I want to lick those unattractive shaving bumps beneath his chin precisely because I'm not supposed to, because it's not ho-hum, because it might destroy his life.) But I've decided the next time he makes that little frustrated noise in the back of his throat, the one that reminds me of Mom, I'm going to try.

I'll storyboard it for him. I'll spread out some of my photographs—of Mom and Elena and Johnny David and Jan and the ones I snapped of Hugh—and together, maybe, fingers brushing, we'll puzzle it out.

The Thing in the Water

The thing in the water started singing to me after Lizet died.

I bought the kitten from a shelter on a lark when Marion and the kids moved out. There was nothing wrong with the cat; she was just one too many. Someone, somewhere didn't spay their pet, and then, when she fell pregnant and birthed her kits, this someone thought: *this creature, this life my actions allowed to enter to the world, I don't want it, we don't have enough room, we can't afford it, it'd be an inconvenience.* So, they abandoned her in a sad little cage in the back of a shelter.

I spent a month with Lizet, scratching behind her fluffy ears and rolling her in the palms of my hands. She liked to sprint across the backyard, and she never tried to bolt for the street, so I started taking her for walks around the neighborhood. She stuck close to me, dancing circles around my feet.

~~~

One day, I brought her to the beach. She pawed the moist ground, trilling happily. Damp grains of sand stuck in the spaces between her pinprick claws. I didn't think she'd go for the water. You know, cat, water.

At first, it was funny watching her struggle in the waves. I didn't think she would have trouble getting out. Animals can all swim, can't they? It's a survival thing. I thought she was doing it awkwardly because she was so little and it was her first time. I didn't know she was in any danger. But when she sunk under and didn't come up, I stopped laughing.

I dove in with my clothes on, winter and all. The cold bit my flesh and the murk obscured my vision, but I found her, eventually. I wish I hadn't. Back on the shore, I cradled her wet, limp body in

THE THING IN THE WATER | 61

my hands and sobbed like baby. She had been my responsibility. I had loved her. And now she was dead.

I didn't know what to do with the body. I panicked. I threw it back into the sea.

~~~

I didn't handle it well. I'd see a cat napping in a window as I passed, and I'd want to break the glass. Children darted across streets without looking, and I had to refrain from grabbing them by the shoulders and shaking them until their teeth clacked. I balled my fists, suppressing the urge to throttle parents at parks on cellphones, parents jaywalking with little fingers curled in theirs, parents smoking with one hand and pushing strollers with the other.

Anger. I was full of it. But I knew it, and I was coping. The singing was something else.

I kept hearing it along the paved pathway beside the beach on my way to the bus stop in the mornings and on the way home in the evenings. At first it barely registered, just a scrap of song wafting out of someone's window. A kid humming, maybe. Or someone practicing an instrument. Background noise in a city.

But it was always exactly the same melody. *La, la, la, la.* A regular pounding, like a knock on a door. Or footsteps. Or waves. It was too precise to be human. And then I realized there were words in the song, and the words were for me.

"Jay," came the whisper-song, in a clear, high voice, like the clang of a key on a kid's xylophone. That was it. Just my name, over and over. *Jay, Jay. Jay, Jay.*

I thought I was imagining it. I thought I was going out of my mind. I tapped the volume on my cell phone to the point of pain and ignored it.

But then I started hearing it in bed at night and at work during the day, on the assembly line between bolts. *Jay, Jay. Jay, Jay, Jay.*

One day, a little girl sat cross-legged on the path. She had dark hair, stormy eyes, and skin that looked hungry for the sun. Something about the structure of her face reminded me of Aria, my daughter, though I couldn't put my finger on what feature it was exactly that convinced me of the resemblance.

"Jay," she said.

I pulled the earbuds from my ears. "Sorry," I said. "Do I know you?"

"Jay," she said, standing. "Thank you for my kitty."

"What?" I said. I looked around, but no one was there to grin or laugh, to point or take pictures of the look on my face. But who would be? I hadn't told anyone about Lizet.

The nearest traffic light flicked from red to green, and cars drove through. A man banged the button for the crosswalk. Two underdressed teenagers edged too close to the curb and rolled their eyes at him. Everything was normal.

"Momma said I had to give it back, but I hung on and screamed until Momma gave in. She always gives in, eventually. Thank you for sending her. I was so lonely before, all by myself, with no one to play with."

I clutched the strap of my messenger bag, trying to get a grip. I'd jumped to a nutso conclusion, that's all. It was all a misunderstanding. "What cat?" I asked.

The girl tilted her head as if listening to a far off voice. "Lizet. What a beautiful name you gave her. Will you give me a name, too?"

"Look," I said. "I need to get going." I started walking, but the girl didn't move. I veered around her. She spun, to face me, but didn't follow. I felt her gaze on the back of my head.

"Do you know what I would really like?" she called at my back.

I shoved the earbuds back into my ears.

I went about my night. I lifted weights in the gym under my apartment. I nuked leftovers in the microwave and ate them in front of the TV. I answered emails. I double checked that I'd put in the right days for time off so that my schedule would be clear for Aria's visit. I slid under the sheets.

But I couldn't sleep. The thing with the little girl's face sang to me, asking me, begging me—*Jay, Jay*—for the thing that all only children want most of all, more even than a kitten.

A Pretty Flower for a Pretty Lady

I heard it in the morning on television, how that girl died at Woodedge Park.

I stood in the kitchen, not yet fully awake, making breakfast. It was Saturday, so there was no rush. First, I took a plate from the cabinet above the sink, next a knife and a spoon from the silverware drawer, then the sugar bowl from the table, and last a blood orange from the refrigerator. On the counter, the single-cup brewer percolated, dribbling coffee into my mug. Sunlight streamed through the eastern-facing windows, warming the room. My fingers slid across the fruit's wet, red flesh, finding its segments and bringing down the blade without thought.

In the living room, the local newscasters droned, voices so bland I didn't, at first, notice what they were saying. A jogger had been killed, her body found shortly after dawn tangled in the reeds that line the shore of Wolf Pond, where I often throw chunks of stale bread to the ducks and geese despite the hand-painted sign that instructs the opposite.

The girl had been a third-year law student. The newscasters said the things they always say. She was an honor student, a dedicated volunteer, a loving sister, daughter, and friend. She was engaged to be married. Her fiancé had been taken into custody for questioning. The people she left behind were shocked and saddened. She'd had a bright future ahead of her. He seemed like a nice man.

I laid down the knife. I wiped my hands on the dishcloth hanging from the hook above the sink. Then I went into the living room and looked at the faces on the screen: the victim's, the bereaved survivors', even the newscasters', but especially the fiancé's. When the segment switched to sports, I changed the channel, ate my orange, washed the plate, knife, and spoon, replaced the sugar bowl, and went upstairs to prepare for my date.

~~~

But what does one wear for a date? I didn't know. True, there had been college, where even someone like me became entangled with the opposite sex. But those weren't dates, exactly. And when they were, I didn't particularly care about making the right impression. From what I could tell, neither did anyone else. Who does at eighteen? Thirty-two is a long way from eighteen, though, and I have learned the value of appearances.

Husbands are messy, brutish creatures. Children, loud, unintelligent miniatures brandishing sticky fingers and muddy feet. But people's thoughts tend toward suspicion, so I pretend. For my mother, with her reptilian skin, alone and grandchildless, gasping to pull oxygen out of the swampy, Floridian air. For my brother and his barren wife. For my neighbor, who is always peeking her head over my fence and her beautiful, promiscuous daughters. For Kaley, my fellow Macy's cosmetician, who sets me up with men like matchmaking is part of her job description. For everyone who drifts in and out of my life, full of expectations.

But not just for them. Today I was filled with morbid thoughts. I often walked through Woodedge Park and loitered by the pond. I was even meeting my date there. I couldn't dislodge the image of the jogger's young face—the color of a bruise and lumpy, as if overstuffed with lollipops—from my head. What if? It could have been. Of course, I thought these things. It is only natural to think them.

As a result, it seemed crucial to gather myself a proper life. Every detail—which earrings to wear, how to style my hair, what perfume to apply and where—became infused with importance.

In the closet, I gazed at the rows of shoes, fingered the colored spectrum of hanging cloth, and felt at a loss. I went into the bathroom and there, looking into the glass above the sink, I knew what to do.

I opened the mirror cabinet, removed foundation, concealer,

rouge, eyeliner, eyeshadow, mascara, and lipstick, and placed them on the counter. Lighter under the eyes, darker in the cheeks, glossier in the lips. A sweet face. A girlish face. A face for first impressions. I smiled into the mirror and was pleased with the innocence and optimism reflected back at me.

I replaced the makeup containers, returned to the bedroom, and all the other details fell into place. Over my head I slipped a yellow dress. The lacy hem prickled my knees. I squeezed my feet into Mary Janes. Around my wrist, I clasped a chain of delicate gold links. Through the holes in my earlobes, I pushed a pair of matching loops. I pinned part of my hair away from my face; the rest I left dangling around my neck. I dipped a finger into an overly sweet and flowery scent, and daubed the insides of both wrists and the hollow at the center of my throat. I was complete.

~~~

It seemed a nice day, so I walked to the park. The sun shone bright and undistorted. The sky spread so cloudless and uniform it seemed someone had brushed on its blue. A deceptively nice day. When the wind blew, it carried the breath of the arctic. People walked around in t-shirts and sandals, fooled right up to the moment they began to shiver. I tucked my fingers into the cuffs of my cardigan and tried to shackle my contempt.

The people all around—mailmen and dog walkers and carriage pushers, nobodies on their way from one unimportant place to the next—annoyed me. A girl had died, and they continued their lives, uninterrupted. They didn't care. Most of them didn't even know.

Was this what would happen if I died? Would all the people I performed the show of my life for scuttle from here to there self-centeredly, like insects, without regard for me, crushed into the concrete beside them?

People like these were the ones who deserved to die. Not the ones who exhausted themselves chasing law degrees or planning weddings or preparing for blind dates. Not people like the jogger. Not people like me.

~~~

In the park, the foliage was in a transitional state, some leaves still full and olive, others russet and withering. The area smelled alternately of the juiciness of newly mowed grass and the aridity of hay. The paths were strewn with pinecones and acorns. Bushes shook with the skittering of chipmunks, but I couldn't catch sight of the animals themselves. Under the faux-Gothic archway at the entrance to the pond, the ever-present flower vendor called out to me, an iris in his hand.

"Pretty flower for a pretty lady," he said. "Free. On the house."

I had seen this man huddling under his awning in the snow. I had seen him in his shirtsleeves. I had heard his foreign accent speaking to other women and friends and conducting transactions. Before today, he never spoke to me. I was flattered and offended. I knew him, but he did not recognize me.

"Please," he said, waving the iris.

It was a beautiful flower: purple and luscious, like an under-skirt, floppy and delicate, like it might fall to pieces any moment. I plucked it from his fingers and thanked him.

"Of course," he said. "It's no trouble. Enjoy." I walked away while he was still babbling, but he didn't seem to mind.

Perhaps people who look but do not see deserve what they get. This man, this flower vendor, orbited the edges of my life and I would have known him anywhere. He was a fool for turning such a blind eye to me. What if I were to rob him? Or beat him over the head with a pipe? He would not be able to say later to the police, *I see her often in the park where I work. She must live nearby.*

I thought of the jogger's fiancé. In the picture they'd shown on the news, he was a handsome man with a strong jawline, thick eyelashes, and hair that fell sloppily around his ears. He looked boyish, harmless, but so what? The girl agreed to marry him. She saw him when he wasn't posing for photos. She should have known.

~~~

My date was sitting on the third bench from the right, wearing a solid green shirt, just as Kaley had said he would be. He faced away from me, gazing at the shore, where a few hours ago a dead woman had floated, lungs overfull with water.

I wondered what sort of man he was. What impression would he make? When he stared into the waves, what kind of person looked back? When we met, what would he see in me? But then, it hardly mattered.

It was like the iris. I would take it home and care for it. I would cut the stem at an angle and drop Aspirin into its vase. I would change its water regularly and place it in a sunny spot. My nosy neighbor with the beautiful daughters would drop in and cluck jealously when I told her about the park vendor. But the flower would die anyway, like all the rest. In fact, it was already dead; it just didn't know it yet.

Hack n' Slash #999

The Beginning

Before: nothing. Now: a field. The grass tickles your thighs. The sky is blue. The clouds are white. The sun is round and bright and hot on your skin. There is a sword strapped to your back. An impossibly, improbably large sword. The sun-scalded scabbard burns the backs of your knees.

You'd like to unbuckle it and stretch your shoulders, but you are not in control of that. You are not in control of anything. You cannot even move your eyes off the horizon. So you stare, getting used to the feeling of existing in your skin: the thump of your heart, the bellows of your breath, the tautness of your flesh, the heft of your muscles, the weight on your back.

There is a noise behind you, a rushing sound, like running or falling. It is worrying, but you can't turn your head to look. For all you know, the world is dropping away, crumbling back into nothingness. It would be nice to have popped into existence just to see this sight: the sun, the sky, the grass.

The horizon is odd. It bulges, almost convex, and the sunlight bounces back to you, as if reflecting off a mirror. If you walked far enough, would you smack into a wall, invisible, but solid? Could you touch it? Your shoulders and neck prickle, as if there's someone standing close, breathing and watching.

The sound behind you changes, takes on a more human note. Someone is making a loud, shrill noise. Someone is screaming.

Your feet move, and finally you turn. There is a house, a huge house, a mansion, and it is on fire. A man is running toward you. His soot-covered skin drips off his bones. The smell of his smoking hair causes a strange feeling in your stomach, like a little man tumbling end of over end. Your face is frozen and unresponsive, disconnected from the horror ricocheting through your chest.

"Master! Master!" His voice is weak and strained. The insides of him, where his voice comes from, must be bloody and raw. He reaches out, yards away. Your feet remain planted.

"The scoundrels, betrayers . . . your family . . . you have to—" The man stills, his eyes blown wide, his mouth a circle of surprise. He falls. Dirt and blades of grass stick to his face. A dagger protrudes from the flesh of his back, high on the left side. The thrower stands a few paces away, right arm extended.

You want to ask, *Who are you? Who was he? Why did you do that?* Instead you grab the hilt of your sword and pull. It is ridiculous and unwieldy, almost as tall as you are and blocky like a meat cleaver. Still, you dash to the attacker and slice her left hip to right shoulder before she has time to fling another dagger. Above the black fabric of the mask obscuring her mouth, her eyes are angry. *Who are you?* you think again. And, *I'm sorry.*

She collapses in blood-sodden pieces. You shake off your sword. And then you do a terrible thing. You squat in the dirt and riffle through the woman's pockets. You take her money, her daggers, a smoke bomb, and a vial of poison. You unwind the scarf. Beneath, her mouth is pretty: pink and soft, like a cherry blossom. You leave most of her clothes and armor, though you do unclasp her vambraces, lovely ivory coils engraved with iridescent, many tentacled sea creatures. You do not know why this is the line, why it's okay to steal from this woman, this woman that you killed, but not to strip her bare.

You move to the other body and do the same, though all you find are a few copper coins. You place the items in your pockets, which feel endless. The fabric does not distend, and you feel no weight in them.

You stand. You tie the scarf around your face, covering your nose and mouth. Then you turn your back, leaving the bodies to rot in the sun, and run into the burning mansion. But when you look back, a quick glance over your shoulder, the bodies are disappearing, flashing and fading, as you move away from them.

This frightens you, but your feet do not pause. As you sprint across the mansion's threshold, blue sparkles shimmer in the air, there and gone so fast you're unsure you really saw them.

~~~

Your feet carry you from room to fiery room. It is misery and terror. Your fingers grasp scorching, iron doorknobs, not impervious to pain, but nigh impossible to burn. Your gargantuan shoulders force open sizzling, wooden doors, releasing roomfuls of smoke that scrapes down your throat and scratches your eyes.

This is not what you would do, if you could choose, but you can't, so you run through the mansion, room after room, floor after floor, head swiveling, beginning to understand that the thoughts inside your head are irrelevant to what your body chooses to do. For you, there has only been the field and this burning terror. But this body has a family, the burning man said, and it searches valiantly for them while inside you cringe and shrink from the flames.

You find the corpses in the basement. Mother and father and daughter face down, hands clasped, heads severed. More blood than seems possible pools around them, staining their collars red. It is gruesome and sad, but in a general way. Nevertheless, your legs collapse. Your knees hit the stone floor and your eyes water, but you can't shift your stance or blink away the irritating drops. So you kneel, fists clenching, Adam's apple bobbing, body trying to master a pain your mind doesn't feel.

~~~

A smudge of dark fabric slinks between the wine racks. You leap to your feet and run, sandals pounding against the stones. Your head swivels over your shoulder, taking one last look at the bodies on the floor as you dart up a set of stairs after the assassin. You wish it wouldn't. Though the heavy cellar door is still closing when you reach it, you can't push through. You bang your shoulder uselessly against it, but it doesn't move forward until it has first completely shut.

You emerge behind the mansion, frustrated by the holdup. After the dim glow of embers in the basement, the sunlight burns your eyes. Ahead, an orchard of apple trees, their branches crackling with flames, stretches for what looks like miles. The dark-clad assassin darts between the trunks, and you follow.

Fire rains onto your shoulders from the canopy and smoldering fruit crunches beneath your feet. If you could stop, turn around, quit, and never see another flame so long as you live, you would. But your body presses onward, chasing the shadow through the trees. The distance between you and the woman does not shorten or lengthen. But she runs and you chase, never tiring, never slowing, never choking on the smoke, though you only have the flimsy cover of the first assassin's scarf to filter the air you suck into your lungs.

The landscape changes. The burning orchard falls behind. It is followed by a flat, prairie stretch, and then an emerald bamboo forest. Your prey still bounds ahead, but now other shadows dart between the shoots. The bamboo thickens, and then thins into a clearing. You shift momentum barely quick enough to avoid the telescoping end of the runner's blade. She flicks her wrist and the metal retracts, like a sharp, glinting whip, back to the size of a katana. You pull your sword from its sheath and grip the handle. Shadows blot the periphery of the clearing, clinging to the tops of the bamboo stalks, as patient and still as insects. The bamboo bends and sways under their weight.

The woman you pursued stabs the ground and leans against the handle of her yo-yo katana like it's a cane. She raises her eyes to her companions, and they attack, quickly, from all sides, with weapons you can barely see.

What would be most effective is a sweeping attack. You need to spin, slashing your blade as you go. You need to clear some space. But you can't. You hack up and down in front of you, turn ninety degrees, and hack again, up and down. You do not have the strength or skill for a spinning attack. So the assassins cut you with their darting attacks while their boss watches, eyes somber above her dark mask. You fell a few assailants, but they are many and you are one, and eventually you topple, belly-up, onto the ground. Blood flows out of you like air hissing through pinpricks in a balloon, leaving a flattening husk as it goes.

The attacks stop and the original runner approaches. She holsters her weapon in a sheath strapped to her right thigh. Up close, her eyes are golden, and her skin is sun-bronzed. She pulls off her balaclava. Beneath, her loosely bound hair is a shocking bright purple. Her mouth is as dark as a plum.

"You die because you stand in my way," she says. "Your family are the rightful owners of this land. But I say leadership belongs to the strongest and the smartest, not to those born into rich families, who suck their silver spoons while all around, those more deserving gnaw the bones of their cats to survive." She crouches and touches your cheek, dragging her fingertips through the heavy stubble.

"Never fear, you won't be alone. Your family is only the first in a long line of those who will know the error of their ways." She stands. To her minions, she says, "Let's go."

Leaping into the bamboo, with her back to you, she says, "You fought well. Be proud and go in peace to your family."

You want to call to her, reach out for her, make her explain. Or tell her that you have no idea what's going on, that you don't know anything about silver spoons or that very specific scenario of people eating their cats, but you are not in control of that. Or maybe you are just too weak. As your vision dims, vibrations shuddering beneath the ground, like frustrated pounding on an elevator button when the elevator won't move. *Is there someone there?* you wonder. And, *Will they save me?*

Introduction of the Love Interest

You wake to the scents of lavender and sandalwood. A blue haze pulses and then disappears. A woman is dabbing your forehead with a wet cloth. Her skin is fair, and her hair is long and straight. Her mouth is a perfect, pink bow. Cherry blossoms smatter her kimono. When she sees you are awake, her eyes widen and she pulls back her hands, placing the cloth in a wooden bowl beside your head on the floor.

You shift on the tatami mat beneath you, blinking eyelids that feel too heavy. The myriad slices you received in the bamboo forest sting under the neatly wrapped bandages the woman must have applied. There are many questions you want to ask. You focus on the most burning ones. *Where am I?* you try to project. And, *Who are you?*

Instead, your mouth says, "How long have I been here?" garbling around a leaden tongue. Or maybe that's just the normal sound of your voice, like river rocks grinding each other down over the course of centuries. The woman lowers her eyes.

"Three days." Her voice is high and soft, like swaying wind chimes. You jerk upright and grunt, pain sizzling across your torso.

"You mustn't tax yourself," the woman says, placing gentle palms on your bare chest. "You'll pull your stitches."

You feel nothing for this woman, this stranger with her huge, inky eyes, but the back of your neck heats, and you understand that your body will betray you in this. You tell the woman your story, or the story of this body and its family, anyway.

After she says, "I'm so sorry," and her voice is full of pain, but her eyes are dead, useless, blank orbs in her face. You would never choose her. She is a simulacrum of tender and caring. You expect an evil spider creature to crawl out of the disguise of her skin. If you could, you would scuttle into a corner. But you can't. So you don't. Instead, you smile, a small, shy smile, and let yourself be pressed back into the tatami.

~~~

You spend weeks with the woman on her sprawling plot of land. In the mornings, you train in the courtyard, swinging your giant cleaver at the wood and straw dummies left behind by her father and brother, who've gone off to support the emperor in the fight against the rebel ninjas, the same who killed your family and torched your home, but for some reason skipped this defenseless manor. No, you have to remind yourself. Not your family. Not your home. But still, a family. A home. And also, there was the humiliation and the fear of lying belly-up in the dirt, helpless and dying. You don't resist this body's urge to improve. The purple-haired woman should be stopped.

So you swing your sword, straining your wounds, every morning. And every morning the woman stands beneath the cherry trees, watching, patient, like a spider in her web. And every afternoon she pours tea as you kneel at her low dining table. And every evening she remakes your sleeping mat. All in silence. This body tries to talk to her at first, especially at night, when she bends over the cot, but it is useless.

"How did you end up here all alone?" you ask.

"My father and brother went to fight for the emperor," she says.

"How did you end up here all alone?" you ask.

"My father and brother went to fight for the emperor," she says.

"How did you end up here all alone?" you ask.

And, "My father and brother went to fight for the emperor," she says. Neither of you change your tone or intonation. Neither of you grow impatient.

Beneath your feet, though, the ground shakes. The waves ripple rapid, impatient, and frustrated, though the woman doesn't seem to notice. *Please stop,* you think to your savior outside the glass, beyond the horizon. *Can't you see that's all we're going to get?*

You are glad when the pantomime ends. It frightens you. Is this body's mind going? Can it not hold information for more than a few seconds? And the woman? Is she some sort of robot after all? After you give up trying to communicate, time passes in a blur of dead-eyed, silent staring and routine.

~~~

One morning, instead of going to the courtyard, you strap on your armor, secure your blade, and gather your belongings. The woman meets you at the front gate, unsurprised, as if you've already discussed your parting.

"Thank you for all you've done," you say, looking down at the top of her tiny, fragile head, still fearing some monster will unzip her skin and step out.

She tilts her head and blinks her alien eyes at you. "There's something I'd like you to have," she says, retreating into the house. Your legs follow her through unfamiliar corridors. She picks up a candle from the family shrine, and then descends, under the house, into the basement. The stone passages narrow, and your shoulders scrape their rough edges, but still your legs follow.

The hallway dead-ends at a wooden door. The woman pulls a skeleton key from her obi and unlocks the door. Though the door is tall and wide, as at the mansion, you must wait for it to shut behind the woman before it will budge for you. The room inside is so large the far edges fade out of sight, beyond the reaches of the little candle's light. But the nearby surfaces gleam and glint, draped in finely crafted, jewel-encrusted armor and weapons. *Rich families, who suck their silver spoons,* the purple-haired assassin said. You are beginning to understand. The treasures collecting dust in this room could feed a village, surely. You look at the woman, paler and more angular than ever in the dim light, and feel a new, more personal disgust.

She places the candle on a table and moves to a dummy. She unbuckles the armor cinched around its frame. You follow and tap your knuckles against the gold-plated mail. It seems sturdy. A stylized hydra is etched into the breast.

"I can't take this," you say.

"Then don't," the woman says, securing the armor to your chest. "Borrow it and bring it back safe."

If you could shudder, you would, at the promise of those words: that you might die or that you might come back to this place, to her. You're not sure which would be worse.

Back outside, you push through the gate and head north, toward the capital, where surely the assassins are also heading. You feel the woman's soulless eyes on your back, biding her time. You look at the blue, blue horizon. *Please,* you think at it. *Please never return here.*

Tutorial: Dying

North of the town, the landscape changes. One moment you're walking through fields, and the next your sandals are sinking into scalding sand. A desert stretches, empty and endless before you. Your body doesn't hesitate, though your toes burn with every step.

You walk. And walk and walk and walk, long past discomfort, long past hot and thirsty and exhausted, long past when you shouldn't be able to continue. But it doesn't seem so strange. You're getting used to this uncomfortable, semi-invulnerability.

The horizon has that glassy and convex look again. If you focus, you can feel the sand rumbling under your feet, slow and indolent, bored perhaps. *Come on,* you think at it. *This isn't so bad.* Which is, of course, when you come upon the gorge.

It is a humongous, jagged tear in the earth. The drop is so sharp, your feet almost walk right over the edge before you notice it. The walls plummet, sheer and rocky, so far down that the bottom is obscured in darkness. The opposite edge of the gorge is far away, thirty feet at least, not an impossible distance, but an improbable one. There is no way around the gorge; it stretches east and west far away and out of your sight.

The sunlight flashes blue. Blue, blue, blue, then stills golden again. Your legs turn and walk away from the precipice, back in the direction you came. *Am I giving up?* you wonder. *So much for justice? So much for revenge?*

But no. Ten paces away, you pivot. And then you understand. *No,* you think at the tank-glass sky, at the sometimes rumbling ground. *No, no, no. Please.* But your wishes don't matter. You lope toward the hole, feet sinking into the sand with every step.

You want to close your eyes, but you can't. You have to watch as the sandy ground shortens and disappears, and the maw of the gorge enlarges. You know the moment your feet sail over the edge that you won't make it. You didn't give yourself enough running space. You didn't build up enough speed. You're going to fall.

You fall. You don't even almost make it. You don't even hit the edge of the other side and grapple with the ledge. Your arms stretch, searching for purchase, but there's nothing to grab.

The drop is long and dark. You try to think of what you should. You try to think of your family, unavenged. But they were never your family, really, and you can't regret. You try to think of the purple-haired ninja, standing smug above you. But she was nice, after a fashion. *Never fear,* she said. And: *You fought well.* And: *Be proud* and *Go in peace.* And maybe, once, she had to eat her own cat to survive. And still she could say such nice things to you, whom she must have loathed for your wealth and privilege. You can't hate her. Even the spider woman, whose presence prickled the primitive, fearing part of your brain, you cannot hold onto right now. All you can think is, *I am going to die,* with your heart pounding in your throat.

You try to summon the detachment you felt at the burning mansion. You try to remember that you came from nothing and that having seen this much of the world is a privilege. To return to nothing is fair. But it's no use. You don't want to die.

You throat releases a roar, defiant and disappointed. It is a relief, for once, to be in agreement with your body. The air vibrates, your beyond-the-glass god trying, too late, to save you perhaps. But it's no use.

You hit the ground with a sickening crack. Your limbs contort improbably, and pain explodes everywhere. And then nothing.

~~~

You stand at the lip of the gorge, unharmed and confused. It feels like no time has passed. No, it feels like time has wound backward, instantly, like a switch thrown or a button pushed. You didn't black out. No one lifted you out of the pit. No one healed your wounds. Rather, it's like the terrifying drop didn't happen. Falling and the you who fell were erased from existence. But you remember it.

Your body, it seems, does not. You turn and walk away from the gorge, double the distance this time. And then you spin and run full tilt at the hole. There's no sense in fearing, you tell yourself. You won't die, apparently. But still, you dread the pain of the landing, the temporary nothingness, the loss of time and experience.

As you lift off this time, a massive shockwave thunders through the ground. You jump, high and far and fast, but you're still not going to make it. Perhaps you'll hit the edge this time, though, and be able to lift yourself to the other side. As you reach the apex of your arc, another shockwave jolts the air, and you jump, somehow again in midair, extending your leap. You land easily on the other side, knees quaking with the impact, but otherwise unharmed. *Thank you*, you think at the sky.

Tutorial: NPCs

The town appears out of nowhere. The heat wafting from the sands makes the air waver. The sparse, weathered buildings sprawl like an illusory blemish on the flesh of the desert, or the saddest mirage.

As you step through the entry post, light flares blue around you, then returns to normal. You are both comforted and set on edge. Now you know, if you die, you will return to this spot unharmed. But also, you might die. There could be something dangerous ahead. Your feet, as always, ignore the wariness of your head, and plow on without hesitation through the sandy roads of the town.

The town is odd. The clapboards that form the buildings are brown, but unwhorled. The cactuses on the sides of the roads are green, but unprickled. The dune cats prowling the scant reeds move in unsettling, horror-movie hitches. The whole place seems flat and unfinished. Your palms sweat. The hair on the back of your neck spikes. Your body moves on, seemingly unperturbed, to the center of town.

There you find a circle of shopkeepers, listlessly hocking wares out of shabby stalls. A leathery woman stands before an array of desert blooms, a flask carved into the wood above her stall. Young men stand at either side of her. One sells weapons: wooden clubs, bronze blades, and a few bows. The other sells hide armor: leather and fur. Across the circle, a teenage girl slumps behind her counter, surrounded by random baubles.

You stop at each stall and have the same exchange.

"What'll it be?" say the armorer, alchemist, blacksmith, and general goods merchants in flat, uninflected voices.

"Let me see your wares," you say.

They push their inventory lists at you, and you drop your head, grateful to examine their goods, for the faces of the shopkeepers are blurry and untextured.

The only money you have is what you stole from the pockets of the corpses of the assassin and what must have been your butler outside the burning mansion. But, you sell the armorer the vambraces you looted from the assassin, which improves your monetary situation greatly. You do not bother to look too closely at his goods; the golden armor the spider woman gave you is more finely crafted than anything he is selling. From the alchemist, you buy a few healing poultices. The blacksmith you only ask to sharpen your blade.

The teenager, the general goods merchant, has only ten puppets in her inventory. The description in the ledger says they can be used to cure paralysis. Your hands close the book quickly, uninterested, so you cannot stop and stare, but the image stays with you: the still little bodies, deaf, dumb, mute, and motionless.

You didn't want to kill the woman with the angry eyes and the pretty mouth. You didn't want to run into the burning mansion or fight the purple-haired assassin and her minions. You didn't want to stay with the spider-eyed woman or jump the gorge or die. But you did, you had to. In the burning mansion, your legs stormed through flames, but your ribs shook with the fear that your flesh would melt right off your bones. There are no strings. You see none. You feel none. Right now, you feel no rumbling in the ground. You see no glinting on the oranging horizon. But you know someone is out there, moving your limbs, making your decisions. You wonder if you will ever be able to choose anything, if there is anything you can do to become free.

Tutorial: Missions

Your next stop is the tavern. The patrons lift wooden steins to their lips with jerky flails of their arms. You try not to notice their two-dimensional faces. As you make your way to the barkeep, everyone seems to be having the same conversation.

"Damn scorpions have overrun the circles. Can't even step foot in my own fields to grab a pepper. Not even one pepper!"

"You hear about Lilly Belle? Poor child was stung seven times. Hope Willard can save her."

"And the smell! Whole place's full of dead foxes. Don't think scorpions even eat foxes. Just killing for sport."

"It's not normal, I tell you. Have you seen them? They're massive."

To the barkeep, you say, "I hear you've got a scorpion problem."

He continues wiping a stein. "You might say that."

You pause. You stand in front of the barkeep, silent and still, for an unnaturally long time. Thirty seconds. One minute. Whoever is in charge, whoever makes your decisions—the ground-rumbler—is weighing his options, you think.

"I can take care of it, if you like," you say, because of course you do. Giant, killer scorpions? No problem for the likes of you. Is it arrogance or kindness that makes you say it? Who is this person you inhabit? Unknown and unknowable; no point wondering.

Tutorial: Companions

And that's how you end up trekking through improbable desert crop fields, hunting scorpions for pocket change. The fields are beautiful, lush islands between sandy waves turned purple in the twilight. The sight is ruined by the sounds, though. All around, you hear the chittering and clacking of exoskeleton and pin-cers. Your hands hold steady on the cloth-wrapped hilt of your sword, and your feet step confidently. But if it were up to you, you'd continue north toward the capital, scorpions be damned. You don't care about some unfinished village in the middle of the desert. But this body or whoever controls it, apparently, is a better person than you.

The scorpions, when they come, after a wash of blue light, are a disappointment after all the hype. They are on the large side, but not freakish. You don't even use your sword; you just bring your boots down on their backs, and they crunch and squish beneath. There are, however, a lot—more and more, in fact, the farther you get from the village. And they get bigger, up to the size of cats, then dogs. You are not sure which is more worrying, the increase in the size of the pincers or of the stingers. Soon you have to use your sword, after all.

Your body, for once, proceeds cautiously, staying out of the reach of the tails, but you are more solid than agile, and some of the pincers scrape against your armor. You hope you have seen the largest of the scorpions. If not, you may soon be in trouble.

As the clapboard buildings of the town flatten with distance, you hear the sounds of a clash: striking metal, muffled shouts, insect stridulations. You run at full tilt in the direction of the commotion, hacking at carapaces as you go.

~~~

You run until you can run no more, blocked by a ring of enormous scorpions. They're as large as lions at least. Their pincers snap, sharp and powerful, like the jaws of sharks. Their tails lash, dripping poison that sears the ground where it lands.

In the center of the ring stands a woman. She wears a battle tunic, lightly armored at the torso, shins, and forearms. It is bleached white, though currently covered in gore. Her hair is short and choppy, but otherwise her resemblance to the assassin that killed your family is striking. Her hair is vibrantly purple, her skin brown. You see no ninjas lurking nearby, though. Her chest heaves. Dead scorpions litter the ground at her feet. She twirls her daggers, one in each hand, spinning blue blood off their tips.

"Is that all you've got?" she quips, diving back into the fray. Watching her is like watching a falcon dive or a marlin swim. She's all speed and agility. She dodges and rolls. She flips behind the beasts, slicing off the tails and hacking at their legs, crippling them, then killing them as she can. All the while, she keeps up a constant stream of blather.

"Take that!" she calls. "Feel the bite of my blade!"

You plunge into the crush of scorpions. The two weeks you spent whacking the spider woman's dummies were not in vain; your fighting skills have improved. You can block now. *Thank the ground-rumbler*, you think, as stinger after stinger slams into your blade. You remove a hand from the hilt of your sword and curl it into a fist. It glows golden, and a ring of scorpions flies toward you. You put the hand back, hold the sword horizontal, then spin, ripping through the sucked-in carapaces as you go. *Magic?* you wonder, incredulous. But why not? It's no stranger than anything else that has happened to you since the field and the fire.

The woman is standing before you, weapons sheathed, before you've realized the fight is over. Your arms vibrate like they're in front of a massive, ringing bell from the prolonged and repeated impacts to your blade. Your legs feel like wound springs, ready to uncoil and hop away from danger any second.

"Who're you?" the woman asks, flicking hair out of her eyes with her leather-clad fingertips and grimacing at the blood the action smears across her forehead. The assassin, this woman's look-alike, would never make a face like that, you decide.

You sheath your sword. The woman bends, rubbing her hands down her forearms and thighs, trying to propel blood off of them.

"The cavalry, it looks like," you say.

The woman slices her irises at you, head still tilted downward.

"Ha!" she guffaws.

"What?"

"Some cavalry!" she says, righting herself and placing her hands on her hips. "You showed up at the end. And you killed . . ." she pauses, glancing at the carnage at your feet ". . . seven scorpions. Not what I'd call a rescue."

Fair enough, you think. "What? You'd have died without me!" you say.

"High opinion of yourself you've got there. Thanks for the help, but if you hadn't showed up, all that would be different is I would have killed . . . fifty-three scorpions instead of forty-six. I hope you've got some altruism to balance out that ego. The mayor of this dust trap promised me a bag of gold for slaying these beasts. I don't intend to share it with some guy who showed up and killed seven, crippled insects."

"I don't care about gold," you say, voice true and sure, untouched by the shame rippling beneath your skull. Ornate tapestries draped the walls of your family's mansion. Lush fields and orchards ringed the property. Only someone who has never had to worry for one moment about coin could ever say such a thing.

"Well, what do you care about then?" the woman asks sharply, adjusting an epaulet.

"Justice."

"Dull," she says, not looking at you, still focused on the leather covering her shoulder, which is why you see it first. The scorpion. The very, very big scorpion, rushing at you faster than anything the size of a small mountain ought to be able.

"Uh," you say.

"Do you hear something?" the woman asks, as the boulder rolls toward her back. She glances at you, and there must be something on your face because she leaves off with the epaulet immediately and curls her fingers around the daggers holstered to her thighs.

"Giant scorpion?"

You nod. The woman turns. The muscles in her back bunch, and she whistles.

"I was afraid of this," she says, pulling the daggers from their sheaths and spinning them. "That cavalry stuff I said? And the mocking you for your paltry kills?"

"Yes?"

"Forget it. I'm sorry. You fought well. Pull that butcher blade off your back and do it again. Keep the claws busy. I'll get the tail."

"What—?"

"Don't die," she says, then runs straight at the beast. She grabs something from a pouch at her hip, a vial, and throws it at the ground. It explodes at her feet and the beast loses her in the burst of glass and smoke. It roars and rears, flinging its upper body into the air, then dropping it back to the ground so hard its feet leave depressions in the grass. You look to the horizon. Is the sky glassier, more convex than usual? It's hard to tell. But then the ground rumbles and goes on rumbling. You pull your blade. Your watcher is with you, for better or worse.

The fight is long and bloody, blue and red. Despite your newfound ability to block and the spider woman's golden armor, the beast's pinchers shred your protection, sawing jagged slashes into your skin. The pain is enormous, so hot it's cold, so cold it's hot, like walking on coals or grinding against icebergs.

The stingers puncture your newly exposed skin. Nine times in all along your cheeks and neck and forearms. You feel the poison coursing through your veins, boiling your blood and clouding your mind, though the power of your hacking slices does not diminish. Despite your wounds, you are not afraid. The pain is temporary. And you will not die. At worst, you will reappear a short distance away, crushing normal-sized scorpions again, where the blue light washed over you, and you'll get to try again, fight better.

When the monster finally screeches its dying screech, the woman stands on its back, hands on hips, smiling like a lunatic. Shallow, red cuts pepper her bronzed skin. Blue blood splatters her like paint on a canvas. Her purple hair whips about her head in the breeze. She's beautiful. You push your sword into the ground and lean against it. She hops down.

"Well, you look awful," she says, still smiling.

"I'm fine," you say. Her smile dims. She rummages in the pouches at her hips. She hands you a vial.

"Drink this."

"What is it?" you ask, palming the glass.

"Poison. What else?" She turns her back on you and bends over the scorpion, drawing a dagger. She chops off pieces of its poisonous gland and some chitinous plates of its exoskeleton. The slices make wet, fibrous squelches. You uncork the vial. A scent emerges, cloying and sweet, like bubblegum. You tip the red liquid into your mouth. It fizzles across your tongue and down your throat and sends warmth rolling through your limbs. Your wounds knit together. It tickles. You drop the vial onto the ground and unearth and sheathe your sword.

The woman stands. "Well," she says, "time for me to be getting back." She pauses, waiting perhaps, for you to stop her. When no words come, she shrugs and walks past you, heading for the town.

"Wait!"

She turns, eyebrows raised. "Yes?"

You shift. "Have we. Uh. Have we met before?" A stupid question. It's obvious this woman is not the one who stood over you in the bamboo forest.

The woman looks heavenward. "Oh, no," she says.

"What? What is it?"

"Were you attacked by black sacks? Stabbed with pointy pointies?"

"Yes, actually. Something like that."

She takes a deep breath, squares her shoulders, and looks you in the eyes. "Well then, you've had the pleasure of meeting my dear darling sister, Kiara." Her eyes skitter away, over your shoulder. "The resemblance is uncanny, I know. Skin deep only, I swear." She laughs, a rueful, self-deprecating whuff.

"Justice, you said," she mumbles. "I've a little *justice* of my own I'd like to deal to Kiara." You want to ask about it, but you can't.

"She's sure to be in Oreze," the woman continues, "lurking about the emperor. I'm heading there. It will be safer if we travel together." She extends a hand. "What do you say?"

Silence stretches between you, on the precipice of danger, like an arrow-stretched bowstring. You aren't supposed to trust her, you think. Her sister is supposed to loom large in your mind. But you do. She leapt at scorpions and shared her potions. You wait to see what your hand will do. Slowly, suspiciously, you clasp her bloody glove with your own tarnished, gauntleted fingers. She smiles again, giving your arm a vigorous shake.

"I'm Rasha, by the way."

"Takahiro," you say. Your name is Takahiro. How odd, not to have known that before. But Rasha is the first to have asked.

"Well, Hiro," she says, dropping your hand. "Let's get a move on."

"Let's."

The woman, Rasha, smiles. "So, what's your transport? To Oreze, I mean?"

"None," you say. "I was walking."

The smile, so lovely, drops off Rasha's face. Two fingers press to the bridge of her nose.

"You were going to walk. To Oreze. From here."

You rub the back of your neck. "Yes?"

Rasha blows out a heavy breath. "It's good you met me," she says, curling a hand around your elbow and leading you back to town. Your mouth protests. But if you could control the curl of your lips, you would smile back at Rasha, brash, and dangerous, and funny.

Tutorial: Glitches

The sensible way to Oreze, apparently, is by caravan. After collecting your coin (which Rasha decided to share after all) and sleeping in the town inn (a strange experience—you lay down and the room darkened, then lightened immediately, like someone spinning the dial of a dimmer down and then back up; nevertheless, you woke rested and healed), Rasha arranges your trip. She haggles with the caravan leader, a leathery man draped head to toe in brown cloth. Eventually, awash in blue, flashing light that no one but you seems to notice, she hands over a portion of your earnings, and then you're off, plodding across the desert atop surly, spitting camels, amid silks and crates and taciturn merchants. But that's alright because Rasha regales you with tales along the way.

"Once," she says, "I had a contract to kill a dragon. A real, actual dragon. Well, a wyvern, I guess. But still. Spit fire. Flew around on leathery wings. The trek I had to make to get to its aerie! The things I had to kill just to reach it! If anyone ever asks you to slay a dragon, just say no. Trust me."

And, "When Kiara and I were kids, we made games of insanities. We climbed trees to nab eagle eggs. We wrestled bananas from monkeys. We stole meat from bear dens. Kiara was best, always. At sneaking, at grabbing, at running. But no longer, she'll see."

And, "There was this man in Vergrine who tried to woo me. Properly, with flowers and candies and lute serenades beneath my window. The whole thing. The clothes he wore. Velvets and silks. And his fingers, so soft. As if I could ever love a man like that. Poor guy, though. His voice was so bad the neighbors pelted him with rocks. They skipped right past the rotten vegetables thing."

And while she talks, she waves her hands and smiles and winks, except when she speaks of Kiara. But you let the thundercloud pass, unremarked upon. The sun blazes behind her, making her eyes glint like coins and her hair light with sparks.

You are happy. You think, *I wish this journey would never end.*

And the world endeavors to grant your wish. First, everything freezes. The camels stop with their hooves raised like furry ballerinas. Kicked-up dust halts in midair. Kiara's lips hang open, tongue curled around an unknown word. You also cannot move, but then you never could, not without permission.

The horizon flashes, like a panicking lighthouse. The ground shakes so violently, you wonder if the earth is going to split beneath your feet. Out there, wherever there is, the thing that controls you bangs on its glass, mashes its buttons, trying to have some effect. But things only get worse.

The horizon, the sand, the animals, Rasha's beautiful face—everything—pixelates and blurs and stretches and skews, like objects pulled over an event horizon, spaghetti-ing into a black hole.

You thought you could no longer fear. You thought the worst thing was death, and that wasn't all that bad. Just a momentary lapse, a chance to try again. But this is something else. This is some glitch in the machinery of the world. And though your limbs are frozen, inside your chest your heart gallops, like the desperation beating beneath the sands. You fear unmaking, nonexistence, becoming whatever and being wherever you were before appearing in the field. (*Nothing* and *nowhere* hisses the fear inside your skull). Now you are Takahiro. You have Rasha. You must go to Oreze. You must stop Kiara. You must warn the emperor. You must stay away from the spider woman. You are somebody. And you don't want to be no one again.

But it's too late. The world rips apart.

~~~

When you reform, Rasha is negotiating with the caravan leader again. You feel a lot of time has passed, unlike your other resurrection, which felt instant. When you look out onto the horizon to the glass or screen or wall that encloses your world, there's something grimier, greasier, more weathered about the surface. And is it your imagination or are there gossamer cracks glistening there? The ground-rumbler has saved you, somehow, and you're grateful. But, perhaps, it took a while and was by the skin of his teeth.

Atop your camels, Rasha says, "Once, I had a contract to kill a dragon." But you cannot enjoy it, not the story, not her animation, not her beauty in the blazing sunlight, because now you have this fear in your breast that you can destroy her, yourself, the very world with a thought. You once felt yourself powerless, a puppet on an invisible string. And now you find you have an immense power that you cannot let yourself wield. You must be cautious with your wishes for they can literally unmake the universe. You long for simpler times.

Adventuring

Eventually the sand runs out, dead-ending into the ocean. The caravan stops in a small, fishing village, and you gain passage on a rickety, wooden, not-very-seaworthy looking boat filled with soot-faced, tatter-clad refugees. Rasha turns sullen among them, clenching her fists and spinning her daggers and narrowing her eyes into murderous slits. You remember the camel-top stories of her childhood. She spun them as adventures, but really, she and Kiara were scrounging for food. You try not to think about their cat, what it might have looked like or how they must have loved it or how far their stomachs distended before they decided to sacrifice it.

Thankfully, Rasha does not turn her glare on you and your shining golden armor as her sister would have done. Instead, she slips coins under the refugees' beds and swims beside the boat, stabbing an overabundance of fish for the galley and not letting anyone pay her for it.

A few days from the capital, a ghostly figure appears in the distance. It grows as the hours tick by until finally you realize it must be massive.

"What is it?" you ask.

Rasha is gutting fish. She stabs a fresh one savagely in the belly. "Oreze's guardian," she says and refuses to elaborate.

When you get closer, you see it is a solid marble dragon. The boat passes beneath it to pull into port. The statue utterly and completely dwarfs the ship. Its legs shoot into the sky, its knees and shoulders leagues above your heads. Something rests in its open, fanged mouth, high above.

"Is that . . .?"

"Real gold? Yes."

"Really? Don't people try to steal it?"

Rasha fingers the wood of the hull beneath her forearms. "Yes," she says. "They try." And as she says it, you hear a scream. A man is falling this very moment from the dragon's mouth. He smacks into the water perhaps thirty feet from the boat, probably already dead from the impact.

"We should . . ." you say. *We should go see if he's okay* or some other such naïve thing is probably what your mouth was going to say. But the point is moot. Some creature's tentacles, black as a starless, moonless night, and barbed grab his corpse and pull it under the waves.

You turn to Rasha, mouth open, eyes wide, a question on your lips.

She shrugs. "Home, sweet home."

You try not to think too deeply about what kind of desperately poor person would attempt something so risky. You try not to think about Kiara's crusade and what Rasha must think of you, sparkling in your golden armor.

~~~

On the dock, Rasha stretches her tense, cramped muscles, and you gape like a plankton-sifting whale while blue light pulses briefly around you. The ground lurches beneath your feet as if you are still a-sea. You hope Rasha doesn't notice the mook look on your face, but you can't criticize the reaction of your body this time; Oreze is colossal and overwhelming.

The buildings rise up, chalky, white, and pristine, like the bones of massive, ancient things. Their accents—the window and door frames, the shutters, the roofs and drainpipes—are ornately decorated, gilded and jeweled. Even at the edge of the city, in this small fishing district, the lean-tos, though smaller than the buildings gleaming in the distance, are solid and beautiful.

Rasha places her palms on the base of her spine and bends backward. Face upside-down, she smirks at you, but refrains from comment. She straightens. "We should start looking for Kiara. We'll have to troll the Brown Quarter. Or the sewers. Knock a few heads together. But it shouldn't be too hard. I'm sure there'll be a trail of bodies to follow."

This seems reasonable to you; you're here for the assassin and her ninjas. But you say, "We should go to the emperor. Warn him of the threat. Offer our services."

Rasha rolls her eyes. "Pointless. The guards won't let you within fifty paces of the gate."

"We have to try," you say, squinting into the distance. You see, very far away, atop an enormous hill, or perhaps a small mountain, what might be a palace. It is so shiny you wonder if it is made of silver or glass.

"You won't be dissuaded, I suppose?"

"Nope."

"Well, then, let's go see the emperor."

Rasha leads you through the heart of the city. It is teeming and detailed. There are hawkers on the curbs and beggars on the corners. Birds perch on eaves and cats prowl the gutters. And there are people, everywhere, moving through their lives. Their faces twitch with life. Their clothes wrinkle and fold, textured to the last detail. Oreze is nothing at all like the shoddily crafted, barebones town in the desert. But its vastness worries you. You feel it's all too much to keep up. You fear the world will stumble, freeze, and rip apart again, maybe this time forever. But it does not. The carts roll on, gliding smoothly across the bleached cobblestones.

Up close, you notice some of the buildings have empty, discolored spaces, gaps in their decoration. Easier to steal gems off walls than risk the drop from the dragon's mouth, you guess. You stop at several vendors. An armorer repairs the places where the scorpions shredded your golden mail, a blacksmith sharpens your sword, and Rasha purchases a rainbow assortment of potions in vials from an alchemist. You also stop to speak with citizens. They have requests.

"Will you slay the spiders in my basement?"

"Will you find my missing goat?"

"Will you bring this healing poultice over to the Nord in the Blue Quarter?"

"Do we really have time for this?" Rasha asks, arms crossed, boots tapping the cobblestones, reflecting your true feelings.

"Yes," you say to one and all.

The last leg of the journey is up a steep incline. A high, rocky cliff, you decide, navigating the wide path cleared up to the palace, not quite a mountain.

"Have you ever met him, the emperor?" you ask Rasha.

"Yes." You glance at her. You hope Takahiro will leave it at that. He does, for once.

Rasha was wrong. You make it to the gates of the palace. You walk close enough that Takahiro can gape, dumbly at them, as he does at everything. They are lovely, you will admit. They and the castle both are made of something iridescent. Pearls or opals or perhaps a metal or stone you're unfamiliar with. You reach out a hand to examine it. Rasha grips your wrist.

"The posts are covered in poison," she says.

"What? Really? How do they wash them, then?"

"Carefully," she drawls, dropping your hand. "Chin up. We've company."

~~~

Though you did not hear them approach, two guards stand before you, in mail and helms as dark as the gates are light. They hold spears whose tips rise above their heads.

"Back down the mountain, continental," says the rounder one.

Hill, you think. "I must see the emperor," you say. The knights trade glances. One coughs, or perhaps laughs.

"Please," you say. "It's important. I have information it's vital he hears." The knights look to Rasha. She pulls a dagger. The knights tense, but she only shrugs and begins to scrape the dirt from beneath her nails.

"What? Are you kidding? The emperor doesn't see any ole riffraff that drags itself up the mountain. Get lost." *Hill*.

You ask nicely. You appeal to their sense of duty, justice, and morality. Then you appeal to their greed. You offer money, gems, and potions. Then you ask less than nicely.

Just when the round knight has lost patience and looks sure to launch his spear through the bars of the gate, the other puts a hand on his chest. "If you're so insistent," he says, "there's some work you could do for us. If you do it well, I suppose we could put in a word with the emperor."

The roly-poly knight flings off the hand, turns, and stalks back to the castle. The one left standing before you pushes a stack of papers through the gate. You take them carefully, mindful not to touch the posts with your bare skin. The knight sucks his teeth, disappointed.

"Prove yourself a knight and you'll be granted a knight's audience," he says. "Happy hunting." Then he too leaves, whistling, duty-free for the foreseeable future.

Rasha holsters her dagger and snatches the papers. She flips through the pages.

"Clear the sewers of muck crabs. Repaint the tomb of the unsung hero. Boring. Boring. Blah. Slay the dragon of Troll's Keep?! Oh, here's a good one: 'take care' of the gray-quarter rebels."

"Well," she says, handing the papers back, eyes glittering like a predator's in the dark. "You enjoy that pointless grunt work, emperor's lackey. I'll be looking for leads on Kiara."

She walks a few paces, then stops, back turned. She sighs.

"If you need a bed, head to the Silver Siren, the big inn in the center of the city. And don't try to be a hero and fight the blasted dragon without me. If you need an extra blade, leave a message with the barkeeps and wait for me. Okay?"

"Okay," you say. You watch her walk away. Why couldn't Takahiro refuse the requests? Or tell Rasha how you feel? Or at least ask her to stay? But you are careful not to wish for things to be otherwise. You don't want to see Rasha ripped to shreds again.

~~~

Time rushes and blurs in Oreze, so that you're not sure if you're experiencing things for true or just the memories of them. In any event, you have many adventures and meet many companions in Oreze.

Jertag, the dwarf, stout and hale with a double-sided axe as wide as a tree trunk, hires you to descend into a collapsed mine in search of a family heirloom. You find the bejeweled tiara, but have to fight a brood of red and black striped tarantulas and their queen, as big as a house, before you can leave the tunnels. Jertag thanks you with coin and a trip to a tavern, where he fills you with bawdy tales and ale that stings your throat.

Elinaria, the slight, fey elf, has a tinkling laugh and shy, downcast eyes, but an acid-green longbow that never misses its mark. She requests your help to reestablish balance in the forest her people live in, just outside Oreze. A sacred artifact has been stolen, a ritual horn, and she must find and return it to the temple of the forest spirits. You help, interrogating the elves of her clan, and fighting your way through the forest's twisted, corrupted creatures. Eventually you must fight a man with a stag's head. You hack at his antlers while Elinaria stings his sometimes-glowing eyes with arrows. Eventually all is set to rights. Elinaria tries to gift you with a burning sword, but Takahiro declines. You're glad; you've grown fond of your blocky cleaver. In the end, Elinaria gives you gold, then bids you farewell, in her shy, reserved way.

There are others: a shape shifter, a mage, a knight of the emperor's guard. They all want something and you do all that is asked. And always, whenever you request her help, there is Rasha, rolling her eyes and grumbling that you are too nice, but still, standing by your side and leaping into battles she doesn't even want to fight just to keep you safe.

Eventually, you do kill the mud crabs and paint the tomb and slay the dragon (well, you think; it disappeared at the end of the fight, but it's gone from Troll's Keep anyway) and take care of the rebels (Takahiro convinced them to relocate, which is certainly not what the emperor intended, but Takahiro is too dumb to know that).

And also, you slay the spiders and find the missing goat and bring the healing poultice to the Nord in the Blue Quarter. These tasks, the ones given to you by the common citizens, are the worst by far.

It's better when there's something obvious to hit. But in the poor districts, in the places where the blinding white stones of the city are tarnished and broken, what good is running errands when the women and men shuffle down the streets on blistered arthritic limbs and the bloated-bellied children dash barely covered in rags or, more often, nothing at all? When the windows crack, are patched, and crack again? Where homeless sit listlessly on corners, dying slowly, abandoned?

A man wearing a tunic made of genuine gold thread tasked you with retrieving a fifteen-hundred-year-old bottle of wine that he left at a friend's. And yet in the same city, nimble, hopeful teens scale the dragon in the hopes of laying fingers on even one piece of gold to feed their bedridden grandmothers. Oreze's guardian, Rasha called it. But who does it guard?

In those districts, where citizens sob when you bring them bread, it's hard to disagree with Kiara. The rich deserve her vengeance. Oreze should be knocked down and built again, better and more fairly. But do you trust her blade to be that? Fair? And does Takahiro?

In any event, tales of the continental and his purple-headed assassin spread like a plague through the city, and soon it is the emperor who calls you to his palace.

The Climax

The night before, you and Rasha tuck into a tiny table at the back of the Silver Siren's tavern. Rasha knocks back stein after stein of the establishment's signature spicy ale, and Takahiro tries to keep up. There is a fire some feet behind you. It warms Takahiro's cool, uninterested back and neck so that you can pretend he is feeling the same beer-and-beauty warmth as you and that you are, for once, in alignment. Though you can't see the flames, their reflection blazes and sparks in Rasha's golden irises.

Some hours ago, she unsheathed her daggers and laid them on the table. They were scratching her thighs, she complained. You have never seen them so close. Takahiro fingers the hilt of one, and Rasha's golden eyes follow the motion of his fingers. There is some terrifying, many tentacled creature sculpted into the steel.

"What is it?" you ask.

"Don't you know? You've seen it before."

Your brow furrows, and Takahiro shrugs, as thick as ever,

though you know what it must be. You've only ever seen one sea monster.

"Why," she says, spreading her hands, "it's the guardian of Oreze, of course."

Your face scrunches into a mask of comical, over-the-top confusion. "But I thought the dragon was the guardian of Oreze."

"Well, it's the one you can see. The bright, white beacon of prosperity and strength. But how can stone protect? And who is it protecting? The idiots who scale it and fall to the kraken? No, the creature in the water is the one with flesh and bone, heart and wits.

"Do you know, the creature does not kill indiscriminately? You can, and many do, swim the waves of Oreze without fear. The creature only kills those who fall from the dragon's mouth.

"You might think then that the two are of one mind. The kraken the shadow, the dragon the light, aligned in purpose. But there is a legend in Oreze that the two are ancient enemies, that the kraken is waiting for the dragon to break its marble shell and descend into the waves. It eats what it thinks are pieces of the dragon, perhaps arms or toes or wing tips. It is misled from time to time, but the kraken waits, patient beneath the waves for the perfect moment to pounce on its prey."

Rasha pauses, gazing into the blaze behind you, looking so unwelcoming, so still and so distant, you feel you are drinking with a stranger.

She shrugs. "Who knows, maybe one day, the dragon will sink to the bottom of the sea and the kraken will take its place, immortalized in marble, and all will know who the true savior is."

"Uh. Right," says Takahiro.

Rasha turns somber eyes on you, then blows the purple fringe out of her eyes. She stands and tosses a few golden coins on the table, pinging the many empty, discarded jugs, and collects her daggers.

"I'll meet you in the courtyard in the morning. Unless . . . you want to get a room upstairs?" She trails her deadly fingers across one of your knees and smirks, almost like herself.

Takahiro looks away, reddening, embarrassed.

"Ah . . . well . . . you see."

"In the morning, then." She shrugs, but a cold dread crawls up your spine. Does Takahiro long still for the spider woman?

Looking into those eyes, silently bleeding flames, you wonder, what does Rasha feel? Is she disappointed? Is she relieved? Is she like you, a puppet on a string, forced to act her part regardless of whatever she may think? Are the thoughts in her head at odds with her actions, her words, her expressions? Does she have a ground-rumbler who only rumbles the ground for her?

You loathed the woman in the shack, with her cool hands and her mechanical voice and her dead eyes, but your body warmed for her. Rasha stands by you and bleeds for you and offers her body, but perhaps she hates you. How can you know? How could anyone ever know?

As you watch Rasha slip through the inn's heavy, bleached wood door, you wonder if you could make her turn around. If you thought it hard enough, could you stop time? Reverse it? Make a different choice? Could you go back to your last flashing blue light and make the world go a different way?

But the ground does not shake and inside, Takahiro is serene. No one is upset but you. Shut down the world all you like, you cannot force the creature outside, the string puller, to change his mind. He's uninterested in Rasha. Does he see something you can't? Something underneath the façade of her face?

And what if you couldn't make the world start again? The first time, it seemed like a near thing. Soothing your disappointment isn't worth Rasha's life. She's here. She's alive and will be at your side in the morning.

No, you will leave the world as it is and live with disappointment as, you suspect, most people do.

~~~

The emperor sends a palanquin, made of the same iridescent material as his fortress. You wear the Spider Woman's golden plates, and your sword is polished and so whetted it could split a boulder in one swing. Rasha sits stiffly across from you, careful not to touch anything.

"Any advice?" you ask her.

She shrugs. "Don't mince words and don't be rude. Honestly," she says, fingering a dagger, "you'll be fine. You're just the sort of goody-two-shoes he'll like. It's me who'll need to guard my tongue."

Two black-garbed soldiers greet you at the gates. They are

anonymous, the visors of their helms closed over their eyes and mouths, though it is possible they are the same guards as before. One is stocky and one is lean. They step aside for you but cross their spears in front of Rasha when she tries to follow. She huffs. The tips of her fingers brush the holsters strapped to her thighs. "Move aside, dogs."

"Stand back, assassin," spits the rounder guard.

"You must have me confused for someone else," she says, as politely as you've ever heard her. "I'm no assassin. Now get out of my way. I've been invited."

"The continental has an invitation. Not you," says the thin guard.

"Well, that's just rude."

"What my colleague means is: you've got some nerve even showing your face here. You think we don't know who you are? You think we'd let you inside the palace? You're lucky we don't kill you where you stand!"

"I'd like to see you try," Rasha grits, gripping the hilts of her daggers, but not unsheathing them.

The tall guard shifts his hold on his spear and widens his stance, getting ready for combat.

"It's alright, Rasha," you say. "I'll be fine."

"You're a naïve idiot." She blows the bright fringe hanging over her forehead. "If you get into a scrap, make a fuss, and I'll come."

The stocky guard scoffs. "Yeah, right."

The other turns his mailed head toward you. "Don't get into a scrap."

"Right," you say as the guards close the gate behind you. They stay to keep an eye on Rasha and leave you to walk the path to the palace on your own. So you walk.

The path is a mile at least. The chalky, white cobblestones crunch beneath your sandals. Ancient olive trees line the road, their trunks swirling upward and their leaves perked, as if turning their noses up at you. Beyond the trees on either side, tidy rows of grape vines roll down the hill, or mountain, as the emperor's guard would have it. Gray, thick-maned horses dot the grass in the distance.

At last, you reach the castle doors. The silver, studded panes are as tall as five men and thrown open in invitation. Blue light pulses as you step across the threshold.

But the walk isn't over. A carpet as deep and variegated as the ocean rolls a hundred yards or more, to the base of a marble dais, up tens of steep, angled steps, to splash at the foot of a bone-white throne. The ghostly bars of its frame give it the appearance of a sea creature, long since plucked to the skeleton by crabs.

The entire room looks drowned. The walls shoot far up above your head. The massive windows are full of blue and green stained glass, casting eerie, watery shadows across the whites and silvers of the interior. You feel like you're standing in a shipwreck. Black-clad knights line the rug on each side, visors down, spears erect at their sides—like silent, sharp-toothed sharks patrolling the murk.

The man sitting the throne waves a hand.

"Come," he says. And so you do.

Up close, the throne is impressive, with sea shells and krakens carved into its arms and legs.

The man no less so. He is dark of hair and dark of eye, with an aquiline face as hard and sharp as stone.

The two knights flanking the base of the throne thrust their spears at you.

"Kneel," growls the fat one. Inside you balk. From the moment you arrived in Oreze, you have worked to make it better, running errands, and slaying pests, feeding the poor, and ensconcing rebels. And what has this emperor done but sit his throne in his lofty palace and order the murder of those who wish for more from life than the chance to plummet from the jaws of a marble dragon? Who is he and what has he done for you or anyone else that you should kneel before him?

Takahiro, though, is simple-minded. An emperor is an emperor, and speaking with this one is all he has wanted to do since arriving in the city. He will kneel. The ground rumbles beneath your feet, an almost lazy hesitance that clouds your certainty. The emperor looks down on you, patient as a rock, neither pleased nor displeased, as far as you can tell, waiting, as you wait, to see what your body will do.

You kneel. The carpet beneath your knees is worn and gritty. How many have crouched where you crouch and begged for land, for food, for their very lives, you wonder. The emperor nods at the guards and they retract their teeth, turning their dark scales back into formation.

The emperor slouches to one side of the throne, resting an elbow on an armrest, his chin on a palm.

"Here stands the mythical hero from the continent," he drawls. "The Sand Walker, the Wave Rider, the Dragon Bane. Assassin Tamer." His lips quirk ever so slightly. "I expected more than a meaty man with a big sword. Wings perhaps. A halo."

In your long-ago battle with the scorpions, magic pulled the creatures toward you and allowed you to cut them down in a spinning cyclone. *I could yank you off that throne*, you think.

"I am just a man, your majesty."

"Don't be so modest. I hear you've done a great deal of my knights' duties of late."

Something about the emperor's tone, some subtle modulation, tells you he is not pleased about that. You feel the shifting of the knights behind you. You fear the bite of metal in your back. If you call, will Rasha hear you? And even if she does, can she make it to you in time to do anything but catch a glimpse of your cooling corpse before the spears fly at her, too?

"A task or two, it's true," you say.

"Why, I wonder, throw down such roots, reach out such helping hands? Is it your desire to be a knight? Is that why you so kindly relieve my men of their duties?"

"It would be an honor, if you'd have me. But really, I only wanted to speak to you."

"Well," he says, spreading his free hand. "There you are and here I am. Speak."

"Right. Uh. I just wanted to . . . warn you."

"Ah, yes. Of Kiara and her minions, no? Don't look so surprised. The city has eyes and ears aplenty and you have not been quiet or subtle."

"OK. Right. Well, you're not safe. She wants to kill you."

"I know."

"You know?"

"Yes. And I knew long before you showed up. Kiara has wanted to kill me since she was a child. Her and many others. Is that your message? Your entire message?"

"Well, yes. But, sir, Kiara's dangerous. She's not just some street urchin cursing your name. She's well trained. And she's got an army. And she's hacked her way across the world, and now she's come back to Oreze for you. Be careful, I guess is what I want to say."

The sharks stir and tense behind you.

"Mm-hm. I do not fear Kiara. Or you, kneeling before me in my home. You know," he says almost conversationally, "there are those who say you are working for Kiara."

And now it is your turn to tense. "What? I would never. She killed my family."

"Did she? It does sound like something she would do, I admit. Nevertheless, you do her work in this city, riling the smallfolk, swelling her ranks. I neither need nor want a savior in this city."

He stands.

"Kill him."

Takahiro gapes stupidly. "What?" he says. "No. Why?"

If this body were under your control, you'd go after the emperor. When fighting a hydra, attack the head and the limbs will crumble. But Takahiro would never. So the emperor exits, cloak swishing as he descends the stairs on the other side of the throne, and you barely bring your sword up in time to parry the sharks descending upon you.

At first, it's not so bad. They outnumber you fifty to one, but they don't fight as one. Overconfident, they circle you, but only one or two at a time attack, slower, bulkier versions of Kiara's long-ago shadows. They jab their spears. The metal tips grind and spark against your golden mail, but spears propelled by the muscles of men are nothing compared to giant scorpion claws.

The ground shakes. The light glares kaleidoscopic through the stained-glass windows. And Takahiro moves as if following the commands of your thoughts. *Block*, you think, and you do. The flesh that shakes with the impact feels like it belongs to you. You and Takahiro and the string puller somewhere out there beyond the cracked glass are united in your desire to keep this body alive. You are not afraid.

When the first spear snaps and cracks beneath the bite of your blade, the knights' jabs become vicious, and the number of bodies in the ring increases. Those outside the circle pace restlessly. Like sharks batting their noses against metal cages, they begin to realize the futility of their actions.

Spears are terrible close-range weapons. And their reach is not the advantage they are used to, as your blade is nearly as long. You'll shred their weapons to kindling long before they get close enough to wound you.

When five clunking knights dart at you, you remove a hand from the hilt of your sword and curl it into a fist. The men jerk into the air. Their spears clatter to the marble floor and they come rushing toward you, limbs akimbo. They halt inches from you, pinwheeling their arms and legs as if to catch their balance. You flick your fingers outward and the men shoot like torpedoes, hitting columns and walls with sickening cracks, then sliding to the ground and lying still. One rolls across the floor, knocking over a horde of his allies. They make a racket like an armful of dropped pots as they tip over.

Huh, you think. *That's new.*

It was the wrong move, though. The remaining knights rush you, spears first, like a shiver of sharks.

Things get hairy. You and Takahiro and the ground shaker lose your cohesion. First one spear and then another batter the weak points of your armor. *This is nothing*, you think. *I fought shadows in a bamboo forest. I defeated a forty-foot arthropod. I slayed the dragon of Troll's Keep, probably.*

Slam go the spears against your elbows and sides, knees and neck. *Slam, slam, slam.* Like a relentless tide. Inside the armor, the blows reverberate, like the aftermath of a bell toll or an underwater explosion, more a matter of displacement than sound.

So, you'll lose. The worst that can happen is you'll have to do it again. You'll fall and bleed and die, pricked and stinging and alone, but you'll rematerialize, stepping through the castle's enormous doors, blue light pulsing. And next time, you'll fight better and win. And if not that time, then the next.

That is what you are thinking when a jagged piece of steel punctures the seam that runs from underarm to hip, slicing straight through two ribs, then retreats, yanking a spurt of blood in its wake.

"Rasha!" Takahiro shouts, voice booming and echoing off

whale-bone walls, out the door, and down the hill to its intended target, no doubt.

The icy fingers that clench your heart are worse than death. Death is nothing. But this. Why, you wonder, would he do that, call her? *Make a fuss, and I'll come,* she said. And she will, you know. She always does. She will run in, flipping and spinning and slashing to save your unworthy life, and she will die. And you will have to watch.

Why did he do it? You behead one knight and then the next and next. Should you end it? Should you will the world to stop? Stop before she gets here and you have to watch the golden sparks in her eyes die?

You wonder, but you have no time to act. A knight hits your helm so hard with the butt of his spear that the world turns to bells and light. Flat on your back, you clench your sword, but are unable to swing it. You can do nothing but groan and writhe on the ground while you are stabbed and stabbed and stabbed.

~~~

The room goes dark; it's like you've sunk to the bottom of the ocean, the sunlight finally too far away to see. Or like a cloud passes above the waves, blotting out the light. At first, you think it's just tunnel vision, just your sight failing as blood gushes out of your veins. But it's not.

It is men and women, shrouded head to toe in black, darting through the room so thickly, they blot out the stained-glass-distorted light as they did in the bamboo clearing so long ago at the start of your journey. It is Kiara's assassins. And striding behind them is Kiara herself. Or is it?

The woman is dressed as you remember: in blacks head to heel, her hair and mouth covered with her midnight balaclava. She swings her katana at her side, like a child with a toy. Twirl, twirl, twirl in her right hand. Then she tosses it to her left and twirls again, no less gracefully.

The assassins have cleared the space around you, and your head is starting to clear, too. Fallen knights ring you as if you're the epicenter of a blast. The assassins form a larger, wider ring around the dead knights. And Kiara is headed straight for the clearing around you, spinning her katana the way Rasha spins her daggers. Her eyes are flat and solemn, but golden, like Rasha's. Her skin is the same cocoa brown as Rasha's. Like Rasha, like Rasha, like Rasha. Oh.

You push onto your elbows and the whole room lists sideways, like a sinking ship. Liquid rushes into your eyes and you blink, eyeballs stinging, world tinted red. Your body sears and aches in a million places.

"Rasha?" Takahiro rasps, like an idiot, spitting blood with his words.

The woman stoops before you to look you in the eye. She loosens the bolt of cloth stretched across the bottom half of her face, freeing her lips. You can see pieces of the vivid hair, cropped jaggedly around her ears. Jagged it has been as long as you've known her, not for style, you realize, but because it had just recently been shorn.

"No. But I did have a sister, Rasha, long ago. Just as I had a scrawny, sooty cat. And before that, parents.

"That was my price, you see, for every lie ought to have a cost, and that was mine. To hear you say her name, over and over, day in and day out, in friendship and trust. Like a lash against my skin. Remember, remember what might have been.

"But now the charade is over, the debt is paid, and I do not wish to hear this name anymore. I am Kiara. Call me as such."

"Wh-why?" Takahiro chokes.

"Why, what? Rasha, the cat, my parents? Because there was never enough—food, water, clothes, beds, money, love—anything. And whose fault is that? The emperor's!"

"No. Why me? Why did you need me?"

"Need you? I didn't at all. I just . . . liked you. The way you fought, the way you moved, how you could be so bright and righteous. Even after I killed your family and burned your birthright, I never saw you cry. You remind me of her, my sister. She'd have liked you."

Rasha. No, not Rasha. Kiara places a vial of one of her healing potions on your chest. "Drink this but leave. Go back to your room in the tavern and run your petty errands and say hello to me now and again when I sit the throne in this room. Or go home, back across the ocean and the desert to rebuild. Or back to your woman, wherever she is. Whatever you do, stay out of my way. I will remember we were friends, and I'll do you no harm."

She leans over and kisses your cheek. You ache to put your arms around her, even though she betrayed you, even though she lied every moment you knew her about who she was.

But then, didn't you as well? Doesn't the flesh draped over your skull—Takahiro's honest, naïve eyes and lips—conceal the feelings that swirl and thump beneath your ribs, the thoughts that zap and flash, dendrite to dendrite beneath your skull? Are you any less a liar? Is anyone?

"Drink," she says, standing, and it sounds like *I'm sorry*. It sounds like *Goodbye*. Because she must know, as you know, that Takahiro will never heed her advice.

She and her shadows move off, in the direction the emperor fled, their treads soft as mouse steps. The room brightens, but your eyes slip shut, and your body goes limp. The vial rests in a dip between the scales of your breastplate, but Takahiro is too weak to reach for it.

At first you think that perhaps that is for the best. But as you lie there, stinging and burning, blood seeping from your many wounds, staring at the dark backs of Takahiro's eyelids, with your thoughts whirling as normal, you begin to fear what will happen if Takahiro dies. Will you begin again at the last flashing blue light? Or will you remain trapped in this cold, dark corpse forever? Game over?

Wake up, you think futilely, because when have you ever been able to move his limbs?

Before the burning mansion you were nothing. But nothing would be better than this. Yes, you'd rather be nothing.

I don't want this. Go away. Stop. You think these words very clearly and you feel their effect immediately. You cannot see, but there's a warping in the air. A sliding. A rending. And then something else. The ground beneath your back shakes.

Ah, the creature beyond the glass. The ground-rumbler. Well, it makes sense. Who would want to guide a creature so far just to watch it die like this: betrayed, tricked, beaten? Pathetic, idiotic, pointless? Maybe you have more in common with the ground-rumbler than you thought. Maybe you are not so different. Co-travelers, really. It the driver, you the passenger. Maybe you can communicate after all. *Spur the horse or I'll grab the reins and buck us both,* you think.

The floor quakes like the world is going to split apart. *Wake up,* you try again. And Takahiro does. Your eyes slit open. The room is impressionistic: watery and fuzzy. Outside the stained-glass windows, light pings and blazes like a thousand meteors disintegrating in the atmosphere.

Stiff and slow and heavy as a statue coming to life, you raise your hands to your chest and grip the vial. The ground shakes so hard your armor rattles as you pop the cork. You tip the liquid down your throat, then collapse again, the glass tinkling away across the floor.

The sensation is as you remember, the sweet bubbles tickling their way down your throat and into your belly. The odd pulling, fusing, but painless sensation of your skin knitting together. The warmth washing back into your body, pushing back the icy wave of death.

You push to your elbows, then to your knees, then to your feet. You sway and have to lay a palm against a marble column to prevent yourself from falling over. It's too soon, the potion has not finished its work, or perhaps it was not strong enough to completely heal you, but Takahiro doesn't care. You lurch from column to column, weaving across the long, wide hall behind the throne—empty now of bodies, the corpses having disappeared while your eyes were closed—until you reach a set of tall, silver doors that match the ones at the hall's entrance. They are cracked and splintered, already forced open. One teeters, partially off its hinges. You shoulder your way through, and the world wobbles blue around you as the cross the threshold.

~~~

Beyond the doors is a long corridor littered with bodies. Knights and assassins both lie crumpled against buttresses and beneath window sills. Here and there an unarmored, finely dressed servant adds a dash of color. A window runs along the right side of the hallway, and outside, the city is in flames, all quarters alike—blue and brown, green and gray, high and low. Black plumes of smoke twirl toward the heavens from the whole of the city. You run.

Staircases branch and arc away as the walls curve and angle. But it is impossible to get lost. You follow the trail of corpses, holding your side, where a particularly bad stab still dribbles blood, barely managing to keep your feet beneath you.

When the corridor widens, fanning out into a semicircular hall, it happens so fast, you can barely process the thought, let alone stop it. You have been so careful, so of course that is how it happens. Your reaction to the thing lying, beautiful and broken, on the floor is so negative, so disbelieving, the walls start to shake and tumble and jerk sideways, rending into zigzag shapes like cloth, like a play's backdrop. Somewhere, there is a smash of shattering glass. Nobody and nothing can move. Not you, or Kiara, or the emperor standing over her corpse. You're all frozen as the world tears apart. As the walls and floors fall away, revealing a terrible, gaping nothing, a void, blacker than soot, blacker than night, blacker than space. From nothing you came, and to nothing you return. *Okay*, you think, eyes locked on Kiara's severed head. *Okay*.

~~~

You reappear outside the throne room's splintered doors, holding your sluggishly bleeding side a millennium, an age, an eon later. Outside the window, the city is on fire. On the horizon, between the grasping flames and the choking smoke, there is a hole in the sky. A jagged, chipped hole, like broken glass. Radiating from the hole, the old gossamer cracks have widened into ridged arms, like starfish limbs. Beyond the glass, you can see a faint shadow. A faint, but massive shadow, humanoid, sitting, and holding some object in its hands.

As before, you run, swerving around the bodies on the floor. When you cross into the hall, you try to slow your pounding heart. *Accept*, you tell yourself. *This is the way Kiara's story ends*. And even if you don't like it, there's nothing to be done. Even if you could somehow throw yourself out the window or fall on your sword, you would only reappear outside the throne room. Whatever decisions you or Takahiro or the ground-rumbler made that resulted in you standing here, looking down on Kiara's beheaded body, they have already been made and it is too late to change them.

It is fair, in its own way. She cut off the heads of Takahiro's family, and probably the families of many others. And in turn, the emperor cut off her head. It is fair. It is just. It is what she deserves. But if this is justice, then justice is only half served. Those fires outside are not only Kiara's. If the dragon slays the kraken, in turn the dragon must be slayed. They are both monsters, not fit to cohabitate with humans. Takahiro seems to agree.

You lunge, slashing at the emperor with your cleaver. He parries with a thin blade that shines like a full moon, so bright it hurts your eyes. It's also strong enough to stop your sword, and sharp, too, as you soon find out.

The fight is hard. You are aware of that. The emperor is no slouch, did not come to rule this city solely through money and influence. He is fast and vicious, kicking, elbowing, and spitting along with his slices. But you are too numb to pay much attention. Takahiro can handle it. The shadow outside the glass can figure it out. You can only focus on Kiara's body in the periphery of your vision. Blood pools around her neck, like a drooping, crimson blossom. Her head is turned on its side several feet away, eyes wide and lifeless, the stump of her neck splattered and gristled.

The clash of metal on metal vibrates up your arms, into your shoulders and neck, and makes your teeth clunk against one another, but you can only think of Kiara, her life and its struggles snuffed out.

In the end, you knock the emperor to the ground and plant your sword in his chest. You feel the metal push through bone and tissue and hit the marble floor beneath his torso. He grips the blade, bloodying his fingers.

"Impossible," he rasps, then dies, still reaching for you, trying to fight back. Well, he and Kiara had that in common then, the absolute disbelief in their own failure.

You lean against your sword and breathe and bleed. You feel lightheaded. You wonder if you will die now, finally. Kiara is dead. Your family is avenged. The emperor is dead, so Kiara is avenged. What else is left to do?

~~~

This is what you are thinking when a woman steps from behind a column. She is like a washed-out, watercolor version of Kiara. Pastel, cotton candy purple waves slither to her waist. Small irises, more buttery than amber, size you up from flesh more cream than chocolate. Her cheekbones are sharper. Her face is narrower and more pointed. No, she doesn't seem like she can be any relation to Kiara, but the coloring bears a faint resemblance.

She claps and giggles, a chilling, warbling tinkle.

"I must thank you, Sand Walker," she says, "for doing me such a great favor."

"Who are you?" Takahiro asks, stupidly, as usual, for a silver tiara—its loops and whorls wrought in the shape of a coiled dragon—perches atop her delicately boned head. The woman chuckles again, close mouthed, eyes crinkled.

"Why, I am Empress Sahar. My husband lies just there, at your feet."

"I—" Takahiro says, then snaps his mouth shut, faltering.

"Don't fret." The woman steps closer, peering down at the emperor's cooling corpse. "As I said, you've done me a favor. Two ducks, one falcon. So efficient." Her gaze flickers to your face. "It's a shame I can't make more use of you. You are . . ." she inhales deeply as if sniffing you, eyes momentarily closing, ". . . strong. Capable. Righteous. Handsome." Her lips curl. "You'd make a good bedmate. Or even, perhaps a husband. But alas, I hardly think the city will love the man who killed the last emperor, hated though he was."

Takahiro pulls the sword free from the emperor's chest. The empress smiles at the blood that wells from the gruesome hole. Though she is thin and weak and dainty, you do not think he is wrong to be wary, to want the protection.

"So, you're not . . . upset?"

"Hardly. My family has ruled Oreze since man acquired the patience to plant his food in the ground and wait for the seeds to bloom. Cornelio and his line were always mad, brutish usurpers. You have reestablished the rightful order."

"And Kiara?"

The empress looks at the beloved body and shrugs. "A distant relative of mine, from a shamed, banished branch of the family who lived as it deserved in poverty and squalor. But she could not accept her lot. I am not sad to see her family extinguished. She'd have killed me as easily as my husband, blood bond irrelevant in the face of my wealth and status."

The empress reaches into the folds of her green, silk dress. Your fingers tighten on the handle of your blade. She holds out a doll. A fragile, porcelain doll, swathed in velvet and painted in golds and silvers. The joints are held together with pins. No, not a doll. A puppet, you realize. An ornate puppet, with spider silk, nearly invisible strings that end in finger loops rather than rods.

"Now," she says, "I really must thank you. This trinket will bring serenity and sweet dreams to its owner."

You remember Kiara's warning that the gates and walls of the palace were drenched in poison. You wonder if that was Sahar's doing. You take the puppet with your left hand. The gauntlet on that hand is more intact, so you risk less chance of the porcelain touching your skin that way. Also, you can keep your right, the strong one, on your blade. The empress smirks at you, knowing, as if she can see straight through Takahiro to you.

"It is just a toy," she says. "If you find it disquieting, it will certainly fetch a high price at any merchant's stall."

Once you stash the puppet, she walks to the window. She breathes deep again, as if sniffing the charring flesh below. She smiles.

"Now," she says, back turned, "I really must insist you go. Leave the city, and do not return. Your work here is done. It will be easy to slip out of the city in the chaos. Impossible once I sit the throne properly and send guards scouring the streets for the monster that slew the emperor, as I must do. So, thank you, and goodbye."

You slink away, fearing some weapon will fly at your back, like Takahiro's butler, all that long time ago. But none comes. The empress just smirks into the night, oblivious to the ragged hole in the sky, as you retrace your path out of the castle.

The End

Sahar is right. No one anywhere makes any attempt to stop you. You wind your way through the city, to the docks. The heat and soot remind you of the burning mansion at the beginning of your existence. Your feet move without your consent, callous to the carnage around you.

At the docks, you steal a boat, and push off into the sea. You don't know how to sail, you don't know how to navigate, but you face the boat away from Oreze, and hope you don't capsize. You don't.

At sea, time does that odd thing that it did in Oreze when you adventured and ran errands: condenses, collapses, blends, and folds over itself.

You come ashore in the desert what must be weeks later, but feels like no time at all. A caravan is assembled nearby, the camels chewing the straggly grass near the shore, as if waiting for you.

The caravan takes you to the scorpion-plagued town in the desert. You eat in the tavern and rent a room to sleep. No one asks you to do anything.

You make use of the repetitive merchants to repair your armor, the spider woman's golden, hydra-ornamented armor.

You set off from the town and walk the hot sands. You jump the gorge and do not die. In fact, you jump the gorge with ease. It's hard to imagine that once this was a task that challenged you, that could snatch the life from your lungs, even if only momentarily.

As you walk, Takahiro keeps running his fingers over the scalding armor, brushing away the sand. And he fingers the cool, porcelain puppet. And you begin to fear.

Somehow you know, deep down, you aren't going home. You won't pass through the lush bamboo forest or the charred orchards. You won't see the burned out shell of your mansion. You won't fix it up and learn to live with your losses.

You will stop at the spider woman's sprawling plot of land. Takahiro will hang the puppet above his bed, and perhaps not forget Kiara, but be okay with her loss. He will return the spider woman's armor and stay forever in her cold embrace. Perhaps you will marry and have children, day after day staring into her pale face, telling her you love her, while she looks at you with her insect's eyes.

Or maybe you will arrive at her door and the world will fade to black. The end. Happily ever after.

Or maybe you will touch the puppet with your bare skin and die, poisoned and tricked again.

Can you allow it, any of it, to happen to you? Will you continue to be moved, a puppet on a string, to whatever fate the ground-rumbler has in store for you? You can see it still, a shadow looming beyond the rips in the sky. And who can say where it ends? Perhaps your decisions are beyond the shadow's control as well. Maybe you are a puppet of a puppet?

But there is something you can do, something you can choose. How much more damage can the glass take after all? If you break it enough, maybe you will be able to walk through it to the other side, to meet your god face to face. Or maybe there will be nothing, just void, just blackness.

Can you do it? Are you brave enough?

Takahiro fingers the puppet, the spider woman's estate hovering like a mirage in the distance.

You thought you didn't care. You thought you had nothing to live for. You thought your story was finished. You thought you'd rather choose death than be killed. But.

Later, you think. *I can always choose it later, if need be.*

About the Author

Carla E. Dash lives in Braintree, MA with her husband, children, and cats. She teaches middle schoolers, procrastinates via video games and anime, and occasionally buckles down and writes.

Did you enjoy this book?

If so, word-of-mouth recommendations and online reviews are critical to the success of any book, so we hope you'll tell your friends about it and consider leaving a review at your favorite bookseller's or library's website.

Visit us at www.meerkatpress.com for our full catalog.

Meerkat Press
Asheville